INTERGALACTIC GOLIATH

He was a gigantic man, about six foot eight, and must have weighed over two hundred and fifty pounds. His face could have provided camouflage in a gravel pit, it was so gnarled and misshapen it hardly looked human. The eyes which peered out at him from the crevices of that catastrophe were dull and beastlike.

The man towered over Deadalus for a moment and then raised a ham-sized fist and knocked him down and nearly back into unconsciousness.

Deadalus's head filled with a scarlet, spinning fog and he barely managed to roll out of the path of the man's boot. He rolled again and came up into a crouch, ready to spring at the pirate who slowly advanced toward him.

"That's enough, Dirk. I want him able to talk."

The commanding voice came over the intercom, halting the giant mid-stride.

Dirk growled with disgust but made no further advance.

"Dirk, you and one of the others search the craft. You other two bring him up to the bridge."

Deadalus was escorted to the bridge. So far, except for the egg-sized lump on the side of his head, things were going pretty much according to plan. They hadn't killed him outright, which meant that someone was curious enough to want to talk to him. And Deadalus felt certain that he'd get all the information he himself wanted while being questioned.

Also by Symon Jade:

STARSHIP ORPHEUS #1: RETURN FROM THE DEAD
STARSHIP ORPHEUS #2: COSMIC CARNAGE

SYMON JADE

STARSHIP ORPHEUS #3

ALTER EVIL

PINNACLE BOOKS   **NEW YORK**

STARSHIP ORPHEUS #3: ALTER EVIL

An original Pinnacle Books edition, published for the first time anywhere.

First printing, August 1983

ISBN: 0-523-41648-2

Cover illustration by Jerry Bingham

Printed in the United States of America

PINNACLE BOOKS, INC.
1430 Broadway
New York, New York 10018

ALTER
EVIL

chapter one

About six thousand light years from the planet earth, on one of the arms of the Milky Way galaxy trailing off the main spiral and out into the nothingness of intergalactical space, in an area that after ten thousand years of human history had somehow come to be known prosaically as J-7, there was a star named *Liberty*.

This star had long been of great interest to that small, and for the most part, unhappy group of men who made it their business to speculate about universal cosmology. All the distantly apprehendable characteristics of Liberty had been so odd and curious that it was one of the first spots chosen for exploration when early inter-stellar travel had become feasable.

Upon close examination it was found that Liberty actually consisted of two stellar bodies which swirled about each other in such a close juxtaposition that they were easily mistaken for one fiery mass. The two stars, which were at the opposite ends of the color spectrum, circled about each other as if in a deadly battle

1

for their one shared name, a battle in which one or both of them would ultimately be consumed.

The twin stars were not near any inhabited planet nor were they on any of the common trade routes, so it was an unusual circumstance that there were two starships within the sphere of their radiance. What was perhaps less unusual, given the nature and history of man, was that these two ships were locked in mortal combat.

The power of the weapons with which the two ships battled was puny compared to the energy exerted by the stars, but it was enough to be fatal to the men and women the ships contained. For after all the thousands of years of mankind's survival, man was still a fragile creature.

Captain Deadalus sat at the main controls of the starship *Orpheus*. The green light of the instrument panel washed over the fine features of his face, giving him the appearance of being under a fathom of water. In the dim light the tightness of his mouth could almost have been mistaken for a smile if it wasn't for the cold, hard concentration of his eyes, which seemed to glimmer with a very different emotion.

His hands were perched lightly on the controls almost like a small bird which, alighting on a lawn, will hop, first on one foot and then on the other as if the ground offered a less stable footing than the air itself. Darting over the switches in short, quick motions, the pressure of Deadalus's fingers seemed much too fleeting to be piloting the enormous starship. Yet, like a cathedral pipe-organ towering over the organist at the small keyboard, the massive machinery responded perfectly to Deadalus's small, but definite movements.

Much of the credit had to be given to the sophisticated machinery of the starship itself. Spherical in shape and pitted all around with propulsion jets, the starship could excelerate in any direction, changing course without turning or stopping. The internal gravity shields were so efficient that they nearly negated the massive acceleration force altogether.

Deadalus fired an intercept rocket, danced the huge ship out of the way of the missile from the other ship, and then fired a missile of his own.

The battle had already gone on far too long. With the unmatchable weapons and defenses of the *Orpheus*, it would have been a simple matter to completely destroy the other starship, but that wasn't what he wanted to do.

The opposing ship was filled stem to stern with precious metal bullion, money which the *Orpheus* desperately needed. To get the payload they had to cripple and capture the other ship, an endeavor which the opposing ship's captain seemed intent on frustrating.

Deadalus tracked the missile he'd fired, trying to judge its effect. Things were not going quite as he'd planned. There was some variable that he'd not known about and it was causing everything to go awry.

The ship he was attempting to rob was an

Empirical tax ship. Familiar with the ships, Deadalus knew that they were equipped well enough to make them secure against the usual pirates, so secure that they were very rarely ever attacked. But the tax ship should not have been any match at all for a starship of the *Orpheus*'s caliber. And Deadalus had carefully orchestrated the attack so that it should have come as a complete surprise. According to his reckoning the tax ship should have surrendered immediately.

But from the reaction of the other ship, Deadalus could have sworn they were expecting to be attacked. And it had better weapons than any tax ship Deadalus had ever heard of.

So now he was using bigger weapons than he wanted to. Trying to use them delicately, trying to just cripple them, angry that things were turning out so differently than planned.

"Successful intercept," the radio at Deadalus's elbow squawked. Followed almost immediately by another voice:

"You hit 'em, Captain."

Deadalus was already aware of both pieces of information. He quickly backed the *Orpheus* out of range of the other ship's weapons and waited. The damage to the tax ship was pretty severe. He watched as the other ship floundered, turning in a slow circle. The ship was defenseless now, and both sides knew it.

Deadalus called back over his shoulder without taking his eyes off the instruments. "All right Jay, let's talk to them."

The communications screen buzzed as Jay attempted to contact the other ship. For a min-

4

ute Deadalus thought that they weren't even going to acknowledge the call, but then the screen crackled to life with the sound that forever reminded Deadalus of the campfires he used to build as a kid, growing up on a beautiful planet he'd probably never see again.

Deadalus turned to face the screen as the image on it solidified. The man that faced him looked grim and haggard and he spoke up before Deadalus had a chance to say anything.

"Why don't you quit playing games, Deadalus? Why don't you kill us and get it over with?"

Deadalus was somewhat taken aback that the other man had known who he was. And he noted that the man had not addressed him as Captain as was customary. But Deadalus didn't let his emotions show as he replied.

"I've no desire to kill you, though I will if necessary, Captain. What I want is your cargo. Surrender that now and there won't be any more trouble."

There was a tense silence as the two captains eyed each other across the empty expanse of space.

"You really don't have any choice, Captain," Deadalus said quietly. "We're coming aboard. You resist, and we'll kill you. Do as we ask and you'll remain unharmed."

Deadalus angrily broke contact.

On board the tax ship, the damage from the battle was evident. The air was heavy with the smell of burnt wiring and only half the lights were working. Underfoot, the hull was

vibrating from the pressure pumps as they
-struggled to maintain the proper pressure.

Deadalus could almost smell the fear as he
came on the bridge where the captain and his
small crew waited. The tax ship had a crew of
seven, two more than usual. Deadalus noted it
as another indication that they had been expecting trouble.

Deadalus approached the captain of the ship
but was met with such a look of hate and fear
that he stopped. The man's eyes held the look
of an animal expecting to be slaughtered. Momentarily disconcerted, Deadalus turned away
to give one of his men instructions on the
unloading of the bullion.

Deadalus didn't like the situation. When people were that scared they were prone to desperate and stupid actions, suicidal attacks which
were unpredictable and often deadly. He kept
five of his own men on the bridge, weapons
drawn.

Deadalus forced his own muscles into a state
of relaxed readiness.

"Why don't you have a seat, Captain," he
said lightly. "This shouldn't take too long."

When the other man remained standing
stiffly, Deadalus shrugged and sat down.

"Seems to me you were expecting some kind
of trouble." Deadalus continued, more to fill
the silence than for any desire for conversation. "Been having trouble with the outlying
provinces?"

"We expected to run into scum."

The sneered reply came not from the captain,
but from one of the crew members. Deadalus

glanced casually in the man's direction, noting the position of the man's hands, the tenseness of his neck and arms.

"Captain Deadalus," the other captain stepped forward, drawing Deadalus's attention away from the man. "May I ask a favor of you?"

Deadalus looked at him, this time not even attempting to keep his puzzlement from showing on his face. There was something going on and not knowing what bothered Deadalus.

"I would like your permission to send a last message to my wife and daughter."

"Why's that, Captain? Are you planning to kill yourself?"

The other man was clearly taken aback by the humor in Deadalus's voice.

"I've told you, I've no desire to kill you or your men. I'm only after the taxes you're transporting. Once we've taken your cargo, you'll be free to go."

"Hah!" The man who had spoken up earlier snorted in disgust. "Everyone knows that the only choice the renegade scum Deadalus offers is between a quick death and a slow one." The man spit on the floor in contempt.

Deadalus didn't look at him and made no reply, except the tensing of his muscles, like springs being slowly compressed. He knew what was about to happen.

The crew member lunged a knife in his outstretched hand.

Before his own men could move or even shout a warning, Deadalus was on his feet. In one quick motion the attacker's arm was broken, the knife clattering to the floor from his dangling hand. Then, before the man's strangled cry of pain and surprise could escape from his throat, he was knocked unconscious by a blow to his head, placed precisely an inch above his right ear.

Deadalus's own gun was now in his hand, pointed squarely at the captain's chest. No one moved.

"I asked you a question, Captain." All the good humor was gone from Deadalus's voice. "Who were you expecting trouble from?"

It was the other captain's turn to display puzzlement.

"Why, from yourself, of course."

Deadalus stared at him with open disbelief.

"Everyone in this sector's been put on emergency standing. But what I can't figure out is how you got here so fast."

"So fast?"

"Yes. From Mewsole."

"Mewsole? What are you talking about?"

"Why, I had it reported to me yesterday that you were looting Mewsole, and that's nearly two parsecs away."

For a moment Deadalus thought that the man was putting him on, but he could see no duplicity in the other's face.

A crackle from the communication screen interrupted him from further questioning.

"Captain, this is Whiskey on the *Orpheus*. We've got company."

"How many?" he asked, simultaneously moving over to the ship's control board.

"Two, and they're coming straight here, full speed."

Deadalus could track them himself now. Two mid-size ships, probably army cruisers were coming along the same path the tax ship had come. It wasn't likely to be a coincidence.

Deadalus used the ship's radio to call to his men in the cargo area.

"How you guys coming down there?"

"We're about half done, Captain."

"Move as fast as you can. And be ready to drop everything and run if I give you the word."

Deadalus turned to the tall lanky crew member that stood next to him.

"Jay, get these men into a lifeboat. I want them out of the way. But don't cut them loose unless I say."

He turned back and watched the approaching ships as the men were lead at gunpoint out of the room. He felt a slow frustration beginning to boil up inside of him, turning to anger. It was as if he'd walked into a trap. Yet he had made certain that there was no possibility of that. He had never attacked a tax ship before. He had never even been seen in this sector. No one knew where he was planning to be, no one but the crew of his own ship. And yet it was as if they had been sitting and waiting for him. It was bad enough to have been forced into actual piracy, but to have some unknown cause effecting events was infuriating. It was as if there were a wild-card he didn't even know about.

After a few moments of tracking the approaching ships, he called the *Orpheus*.

"Whiskey? Here's the plan, they look like army cruisers, shouldn't be too much trouble. What I want you to do is to wait until they get in visual range, then take off as if you're trying to run. But keep this ship between you and them. They won't figure on being shot at by their own team. Be ready to turn back as soon as I start shooting. OK?"

"Got it, Captain. But how come I don't just take them out with the *Orpheus?*"

"Just do as I say," Deadalus snapped, and then broke contact.

Whiskey's suggestion bothered him because he knew that it would be simpler and easier than what he himself had planned. But Deadalus just couldn't bring himself to sit by idle. He felt as if things had been sneaking up behind him all day, and that everytime he turned around to fight back there was nothing there. Now he had an identifiable foe and he wanted to act, to strike out. He wanted to show that he was in control again.

He looked over the instrument panel while he waited for the ships to get close. The tax ship of Earth construction and so the panel was extremely similar to the *Orpheus*'s. Deadalus was familiar with most major ship constructions, and could, in a pinch, pilot any of them. That had all been a part of his secret police training.

He thought back now on those long years of training with a disgust that bordered on fury. From his twelfth year on they had schooled him, indoctrinated him, shaped and molded him, all toward the end of forming him into an expert killer, an organic weapon to be used by the Empirical government.

Well, they had succeeded into making him

10

into a superb weapon, almost undefeatable. Only now he was working against them, not for them.

As the cruisers sped closer, they veered apart and Deadalus suddenly realized what a foolish risk he was taking. He was in a ship that he himself had disabled, yet had no idea to what extent. He was gambling on them not knowing he was on the ship. But he really didn't know what they knew. He wasn't at all certain what was going on.

For a fleeting moment he even thought of calling Whiskey with a change of plans. But it was already too late. The cruisers were too close and they'd pick up any radio message.

His mind became clear and sharp, free from any interfering emotions, the well-trained awareness that he went into whenever in a dangerous situation. He knew he had had no right to gamble with others lives as if they were merely chips in a card game, but he'd worry about that later. Right now he had to concentrate on getting them out of the situation he'd so irresponsibly gotten them into.

As the two ships got into visual range, Deadalus watched as Whiskey played the bluff brilliantly. First he fired a short laser burst in the direction of approaching ships, a shot which gave away his location, making certain that the cruisers saw him. Then, with a sort of hesitant motion, the *Orpheus* took off, keeping the tax ship between itself and the other ships. Deadalus could tell that Whiskey was not pushing the *Orpheus* to anything near full speed, but, he realized, the chasing ships would not know that. And this way, the *Orpheus* would be much closer if something went wrong.

Deadalus noted how Whiskey's improvisations improved upon the orders he'd been given, and, though Deadalus was pleased with the young man's quick thinking, he was not pleased that he had given orders which could be easily improved upon.

Deadalus cleared his mind of all extraneous thoughts, becoming as near as possible an extension of the ship's weapons' system. His hands rested lightly on the instruments and his eyes watched the dials with unflinching concentration. The next few seconds would show if they were going to fall for the bluff or not.

The two army cruisers, for that was now clearly what they were, spotted the *Orpheus* immediately and veered toward it. One of the ships immediately increased speed to give chase, but the other ship hesitated as if undecided whether to chase the *Orpheus* or to investigate the tax ship. Deadalus's hand steadied on the firing button.

The cruiser decided. It increased its speed and swerved around the stationary tax ship. The bluff worked perfectly. In a moment both cruisers were close alongside the tax ship, one on either side.

Deadalus grinned and fired. He could have hit them with his eyes closed. Mere child's play.

That is, if decimating spaceships and their crews wasn't a game reserved solely for adults.

The *Orpheus* reversed direction the instant Deadalus fired, but its assistance wasn't needed.

"How's the unloading coming?" Deadalus called down to the cargo area.

"We've nearly got it all," an excited voice answered. "Man, you wouldn't believe all the stuff they've got here! There's all sorts of jewels and . . ."

"Just pack it up," Deadalus snapped, stopping the other's lighthearted excitement as suddenly as if he'd struck him.

Deadalus wanted to get off the ship as quickly as possible. Those two army cruisers had not happened by coincidentally. They had been expecting trouble. And if the trouble they were expecting was the *Orpheus*, then there would be a lot more than just two ships waiting.

As if in response to his thoughts, three more enemy ships appeared on the tracking screen.

"Everyone back to the *Orpheus*" he called over the PA system, hitting the attack alarm. "Whiskey, stand by to pick us up."

As he turned to hurry out of the control room Deadalus saw two more enemy ships appear on the screen. They weren't going to be able to bluff their way out of this one.

The *Orpheus*'s three landing crafts got back to the ship just as the first of the attackers got within firing range. Whiskey successfully fended it off and, by the time the second ship attacked, Deadalus had taken the controls back from his second in command.

The smaller, less powerful cruisers were all over the *Orpheus*, like a pack of dogs on a bear. The well-trained crew of the *Orpheus* was able to fend off the attacking ships but, having to keep its attention on all five of them, the *Orpheus* was unable to do any extensive damage to them.

Deadalus battled with them for a few minutes, knowing he wasn't going to be able to defeat them, and looked for an avenue of escape. Finally he spotted an opening and shot the *Orpheus* toward it.

One of the cruisers sped over to try and head him off but Deadalus knew that the *Orpheus* was too fast. Deadalus also saw that, in trying to cut him off, the other ship had overshot its cover and was vulnerable to attack.

Jumping at the opportunity, Deadalus changed the *Orpheus*'s course suddenly, turning away from the obvious line to freedom. The cruiser tried to adjust, but there wasn't time. In half a breath the *Orpheus* was underneath it, and in the next moment there was a brilliant orange ball of flame where the cruiser had been.

The whole maneuver took only a moment, but Deadalus immediately knew he had made a mistake. The time he'd wasted in attacking the cruiser was enough to let two other ships catch up with him.

Deadalus slammed the *Orpheus* into full speed and at the same moment felt a dull thud vibrate through the ship. He knew they'd been hit. A moment later a scattering of warning lights blinked on the control panel and he knew the damage was serious.

He kept the ship on full throttle. In a few

minutes he'd outdistanced the cruisers. In another minute the *Orpheus* was even beyond their tracking range. He changed courses but didn't slow down.

There were emergency sirens wailing through the ship now and the control panel indicated an imminent breakdown. Still Deadalus didn't slow down. He wanted to get as far away from this sector as possible before the ship stopped.

Five minutes passed. Someone had shut off the emergency siren. Deadalus's full concentration was on piloting the starship as it swept through space like some kind of half-crazed comet.

With a jolt, half of the ship's power went out. They started spinning and Deadalus shut down the other engines and sat back. Everything seemed suddenly quiet. Faintly, Deadalus could hear the air-circulation system, puffing like an overweight man running up hill. Whiskey was staring at him questioningly, but Deadalus avoided meeting his gaze.

"Captain, this is engine room two. Things don't look real good down here."

"Be precise!" Deadalus unsuccessfully tried to keep the edge out of his voice.

"We've sealed off the air leak, but the thing that goes between the power supply and the engine line is pretty messed up."

"You call that precise? What kind of engineer are you? Listen, Wilson, if you don't start doing better than that . . ."

"Sir, this isn't Wilson," the voice over the

radio interrupted him. "This is Rawlings from communication."

"Rawlings? Where the hell's the engineer Wilson? Get him on."

"I'm afraid I can't, sir. He's dead."

chapter two

Deadalus sat alone in his cabin. Perched on the edge of his bunk he peered down at the floor, his eyes as hard and sharp as a falcon's looking for prey. A dark cloud of emotion played across his arian features.

He was not accustomed to losing men. It would happen now and then, it couldn't really be avoided. But this was the first time that it had happened due to a mistake by Deadalus himself. He had let his emotions interfere with his judgment. He had succumbed to his anger and struck out when he should have backed off. Consequently, a man had unnecessarily lost his life, a man who, like all the crew, had been completely dependent on Deadalus not making stupid mistakes.

Deadalus longed to work alone, like he had when he was with the secret police. There had been a sort of freedom in knowing that the only neck he risked was his own.

The Empirical secret police force had been set up at the end of the great war. The military council of Earth, which now called them-

17

selves "the Empirical Government," had wanted to insure that all the farflung galactical colonies stayed in line. These societies, which had been completely independent and isolated during the thousands of years of the third dark ages, did not submit willingly to the domination of Earth. But as long as Earth maintained an exclusive hold on all technological and weapon development there was not much that the people on the other planets could do.

The secret police played a major role in this oppression. Completely outside of the law they operated undercover, spying, subverting, and destroying.

Deadalus had been one of the top agents and probably would have continued so if it hadn't been for his uncle, who was the chief of the secret police. Deadalus was representative of a new, younger generation, with new lifestyles and beliefs. Chief Hissler, his uncle, was old, dictatorial, overbearing, and spiteful. The older man could not stand Deadalus's disrespectful attitude toward the government and, despite the necessity of their working relationship, they could never get along. Still, things might have gone on like that for a long time if Deadalus hadn't started questioning the policies of the secret police.

At first it was just the method that he disagreed with. Deadalus had no qualms about the use of force for keeping order; history had long shown it to be the only viable method. But it seemed to him inexcusably unprofessional to use more force than necessary. The Chief seemed to encourage indiscrimanent de-

struction. Many of the agents routinely killed
dozens of people, when the job could have been
done with few, if any, deaths. Deadalus thought
it was sloppy ånd didn't hide his feelings. To
press his point further, he worked in the opposite manner. He would analyze the situation
and determine the precise spots where the least
amount of pressure needed to be applied to get
the job done. His uncle told everyone that
Deadalus was just lazy, but it soon became
known that there was no other agent on the
force who could match Deadalus's efficiency.

Still, things would not have come to a head
if Deadalus hadn't started questioning the goals
as well as the methods.

Like everyone else, Deadalus had been fully
indoctrinated to believe that the Empirical Government was the very best thing for the entire
galaxy and, therefore, anything that hurt the
government hurt the people as well. But more
and more Deadalus became aware that the
Empirical Government was really a matter of
oppressing the great majority for the benefit of
a select few. And the politicians covered up
what they were doing in the best Machiavelian
manner, using so much doubletalk and sophisticated reasoning, that the great majority of the
people didn't even realize they were being taken
for a ride.

As Deadalus voiced his disillusionment, the
friction between him and his uncle, the Chief,
grew to the point that sparks flew whenever
they met, constantly threatening to blaze out
of control.

Finally, his uncle had sent him on an assignment which was just more than he could swallow. Deadalus said it was wrong. Chief Hissler said to do it or else. Deadalus said he quit. His uncle said that was fine, and then assigned an agent to assassinate him.

When Deadalus found that his uncle wanted him dead, he decided to fight back. In a surprise move, he was able to take over one of the secret police's starships. He gathered together a crew from among the young political disidents and trained them into a superb fighting force.

His uncle had branded him as a killer and bandit, but there was an ever-growing number of people who knew otherwise and helped Deadalus and the crew of the *Orpheus* whenever they could.

And now, for the first time he could remember, one of his crew had died because Deadalus had made a mistake. Sitting on his bunk, Deadalus looked at his hands as if they held the secret of bringing the dead back to life. Finally, with a sudden movement as if tearing himself away, Deadalus got up and went to talk to Whiskey who, he knew, would be waiting for him with a full report on the damage to the ship.

The loud argument stopped mid-breath as Deadalus strode into the navigation room. He looked with some surprise at the two flushed faces of the arguers.

Whiskey sat at one side of the long, narrow chart table, clutching a writing pad with such force it was in imminent danger of breaking.

He was shorter and stockier than Deadalus, with a young, square face topped with a toss of red hair. His mouth was tight with the effort of containing his anger.

Standing across from him on the far side of the table, her fists on her small hips and her feet planted as if ready for a brawl, Rhea returned Whiskey's glare with equal ferociousness. Dark, shoulder-length hair framed the features of her face which, on a normal occasion, were quite pretty. Right at the moment however, her appearance was dominated by the thrust of her chin, a chin which had the mark of someone who never backed down.

Deadalus looked back and forth between the two. It was not the fact that they were arguing which surprised him, that was the normal state of affairs. Rhea, who was stubbornly idealistic, was constantly infuriated by Whiskey's pretentious air of worldly cynicism, knowing that underneath he was as idealistic as herself. Whiskey, for his part, was always grumbling that Rhea, who was a brilliant scientist, lacked all mechanical sense of what was possible and what impossible, and was always designing things for him to build without any consideration of the fact that he didn't have access to half the pieces she called for. But their arguing had always been like the banter of a brother and sister who knew that when the chips were down, they'd stand up for each other against all odds. It was the unqualified anger flushing their faces which surprised Deadalus. That, and the fact that they stopped as soon as he came in.

Neither Whiskey or Rhea would meet his questioning gaze, so Deadalus looked at the only other person in the room, Jay.

Jay was sitting at the far end of the table, his long loose form dropped casually in a chair, a pleasant, impenetrable expression on his face. As usual, Jay seemed completely unconcerned. Even in the midst of the most trying circumstances, Deadalus had rarely seen him display his feelings. He met Deadalus's questioning look with a smile and a small shrug.

Deadalus was about to ask what the trouble was, but then changed his mind.

"What's the report on the damage?" he asked instead, sitting down across from Whiskey.

Whiskey cleared his throat and looked down at the writing pad he held.

"It looks pretty bad. I don't have the information on the outer skin yet, but there's a ten-foot hole in the third layer. As far as the engine itself, the major damage is to the transmission drive and the fuel exchanger."

"How severe is it?"

"They're completely out of commission."

Deadalus sighed and ran his hand through his hair. "How long do you think it will take to fix them?"

"I could probably have the fuel exchanger working in a couple days, but it would take cannabalising one of the landing crafts. But the transmission drive is beyond repair. It'll have to be replaced."

Deadalus knew that Whiskey's knack for working with anything mechanical or electrical was equal to the best technician anywhere.

The young man was able to get things working long after everyone else had given up. If Whiskey said something was unrepairable Deadalus was willing to take his word for it.

"And there's nothing on board that we could replace it with, even temporarily?" Deadalus asked, though he already knew the answer just by the look on Whiskey's face.

"Not a thing, Captain. I don't really think you could substitute for it anyways. It's too precise and too essential of a component."

Deadalus waited for the young man to continue, but he was evidently through with the report. He thought a moment and then turned to Jay.

"Did you get a count on what we got from the tax ship?"

"Well, they're still trying to get a full count, but I went through and got a rough idea. If it were converted to Empirical currency it would be about half-a-billion pounds. It's a bit difficult to be precise though. As well as the metal buillion, there's nine different currencies and a couple crates of jewels, both rough-cut and polished. I've no idea of their value, so I didn't figure them in."

There was a low whistle from Whiskey and Jay smiled.

"It's enough to retire on, Captain."

Deadalus flinched at the remark and turned around to look at Rhea. She had been pacing behind him and now stopped as he looked at her.

"Did it go alright?"

Rhea shrugged, met his gaze for a moment, then looked away.

"There wasn't anyone on the files to contact. We gave him a space burial."

Rhea had been in charge of seeing to the burial of the crew member. A space burial was a rather unsentimental affair. The body was simply cremated in the incinerator compartment of the heating room and then dumped into space out the waste chute. As inglorious as this seemed, it was the way everyone who died in space was buried. That is, those who were lucky enough to be buried.

"Did you notify his home planet?" Deadalus watched her closely, trying to see what exactly was bothering her.

"No." She started to say something more, but stopped, apparently trying to regain control of herself.

"Why not?"

"Because I didn't know what to say." She glared, her voice seeping with bitterness. " 'Killed while pirating an Empirical government ship' did not seem quite appropriate."

Whiskey spoke up before Deadalus had a chance to reply.

"You could have said he died while defending the freedom of man."

"If I was going to make something up, I would think of something a little more believable," Rhea sneered back.

"What's the matter, Rhea?" Deadalus spoke a little sharper than he'd intended. "Do you suddenly find that what we're doing isn't worth dying for? You want that we should just find some nice safe little planet and keep out of the way?"

"Just what exactly is it that we are doing? I thought we were fighting against people like Hissler because they were a bunch of murderers and thieves who were concerned only with their own gain. What sense does it make if we start doing the same thing as them?"

Whiskey leaped to his feet, extremely agitated.

"You don't mean to say that you think that this tax money rightfully belongs to the government, do you?"

"No. But it doesn't belong to us either!"

"Just how do you propose we keep the *Orpheus* running?" Deadalus asked, his voice as cold as the empty space between stars.

"I don't know. But it sure doesn't make any sense doing it this way."

"Speaking of keeping the *Orpheus* running," Jay's slow drawl interrupted the heated discussion. "Just what is the plan, Captain?"

Deadalus forced himself to ignore his rising irritation and get back to the problem at hand.

"All right. According to the charts, there are three colonized planets fairly close by. Since, as Jay told us, we have quite enough money, it seems the best idea would be to just go and buy everything we need. One of the planets is off in a different direction from the other two, so we'll send two landing crafts, to save time. Rhea, you take one, and I'll be in charge of the other. Any questions?"

He looked at Rhea and Whiskey; they both just shook their heads. Then Jay spoke up.

"Yeah, Captain. What do you suppose that other captain meant when he said he'd heard we were in the area, looting planets?"

Deadalus shrugged, trying to look unconcerned.

"I don't know Jay, just another crazy rumor."

But even as he nonchalantly dismissed the subject, Deadalus knew that he hadn't heard the last of it.

chapter three

Deadalus wiped his hand across his face again. His clothes were soaked from the sweat, which seemed to just pour off him. He felt as if he'd fallen into a deep and salty sea.

He looked at the three crewmen he'd brought with him into the town. They were standing talking with a group of the locals at the side of the small supply shop. Nervously, Deadalus flexed his calf muscle, feeling the security of the weapon he'd concealed in his boot.

The machine parts clerk came back with the pieces of equipment that Deadalus had ordered.

"Can I get you anything else?"

"Yeah, I was wondering if you could cut this part for me." Deadalus handed him a computer generated diagram of the transmission drive. "How long do you think it'll take?"

The man looked over the specifications.

"Oh, ten minutes at the most."

One of Deadalus's men casually walked over as the clerk took the printout into the other room to be cut.

"Be going pretty soon, Captain?"

"Ten minutes. Why?"

"Oh, just thought you might want to chat with some of the local boys over there."

Deadalus sensed that the casualness of the man's voice was forced.

"What's up?" Deadalus glanced at the knot of men. They were discussing something with animation, but there didn't seem to be anything threatening in their attitudes.

"They've been telling us about some rogue named Deadalus who's been terrorizing the area. And they're quite explicit about what they're going to do to him when they catch him."

"That right?" A few of the locals were eyeing him so Deadalus smiled, friendly. "Going to throw him a welcoming party, are they?"

"Yeah. A real bar-b-que."

Still smiling, Deadalus walked over to the group of local residents. He didn't want to aggrevate the situation but he was too intrigued to pass up the opportunity to find out more about this rumor.

"Been having trouble with pirates hereabouts?" he asked the group of men.

"Surprised you haven't heard." It was one of the older fellows who spoke up. "This pirate Deadalus has looted five planets in this sector alone. He's too much for the local police forces, the way the damn government keeps them nearly helpless with all the weapon restrictions. And the army can't seem to catch up with him."

"Looted five planets?" Deadalus had to fight to keep the smile from his face. "That's a bit difficult to believe. Sounds a bit like a wild rumor to me."

"Rumor hell! The army had over a hundred refugees here last week. And if you think it's an exaggeration, you just should have seen their faces when they talked about it. You wouldn't have had no doubts then, that's for sure."

"What did they say?"

"Just that his men took whatever they wanted, killed anyone who got in their way, raped half the women and abducted nearly two dozen of them. We've been half expecting him to show up here at any time."

"We don't got nothing for him here," a second man added quickly.

"He's probably long gone by now," someone else added, but with little conviction.

"No one knows," the first speaker corrected. "No one really knows anything about him."

"Still," Deadalus said, trying to keep the conversation limited to the facts, "five planets, that's kind of hard to believe. You talk as if he has a whole task force."

"He's got two ships. They're old army cruisers that he's converted to power-drive. And the crews are a bunch of killers who have nothing left to lose."

While the older man was talking, there came in from the street three other men who pushed their way to the front of the small crowd which had gathered around Deadalus and his men.

The apparent leader of these three newcomers was an enormous man, hugely muscled. Though in his youth the man must have been the toughest kid on the block, his muscles had gone to seed, slack and untoned. Had he been a side of beef he would have been all pot-roast.

Deadlus took one look at the man's face and knew that he was going to cause trouble. The man had the look of a town bully, with two, small black eyes set down close beside a nose that would have looked good on a bull-dog.

"Just let him try and come here!" the man smirked. "He ain't gonna find us rolling over and playing dead for him. I'll tell you that!" He glared at Deadalus as if daring him to contradict him.

"I'm surprised you haven't heard about him," the older man said.

"I have heard about this Deadalus character before," Deadalus admitted. "But I never heard of him having two ships, nor of doing the kind of things you've mentioned. How do you know it's the same guy?"

"Oh, everyone knows. Fact is, he seems to go around bragging about it."

Deadalus thought about that for a moment.

"That's kind of peculiar, isn't it? Why would a pirate go around telling everyone who he is?"

"He isn't your normal pirate, that's for sure." The old man shook his head. "Some say he's designing to set up his own, separate kingdom."

The big newcomer scoffed.

"He's got a second thought coming to him if he thinks he's going to get me to meekly submit." He looked at Deadalus challengingly.

Deadalus ignored him.

"What exactly is he after?"

"Just about anything. Money, food, jewels, women."

"Women!" Deadalus laughed despite himself. "What does he do with the women?"

"No one knows. Some say when he's done with them he just throws them away. Others say he's got a hideout somewhere. All I know is that no one's ever come back to tell about it."

Deadalus looked about at the crowd of men who were shaking their heads in grim agreement with the old man. Beyond them the street outside shimmered in the heat, as if it were melting away. Even inside, in the supposedly climate-controlled store, the heat was nearly unbearable.

"And what does the army say?" Deadalus asked, still trying to make some sense out of the information they'd just given him.

"You sure do ask a lot of questions," the overweight man said before the older man could reply.

Deadalus looked at him steadily.

"If there's a pirate in the area it makes sense for me to find out all I can, doesn't it?"

"Sure. Except your men here said you was transporting second grade ore. This pirate ain't likely to be interested in that."

"Not likely," Deadalus replied as patiently as he could. "But I wouldn't want him stopping me to find out."

The clerk had finished cutting the piece and Deadalus now wanted to bring the conversation to a swift conclusion. He knew that, given enough time, the young guy would find some way to make trouble.

"What are you doing transporting ore in this area, anyways?" the man continued as Deadalus paid for the things he had purchased.

"I didn't intend to be. We had a fire in one of the compartments. The load shifted as we trying to put it out. It wrecked one of the engine rooms." He picked up the piece and prepared to leave. He was pretty good at making up stories on the spot, but he wasn't sure how much scrutiny this one would stand up to. And he didn't really want to hang around to find out.

The overweight troublemaker stood in Deadalus's path, showing no intention of moving.

"That doesn't sound real likely to me. In fact, there's a lot of things about you I don't like."

Deadalus smiled at him, not quite pleasantly.

"I got clearance from your port authority," he lied. "If you've got any questions, take it up with them."

"I just might do that. And maybe you'll just stick around until I do."

The crowd shifted slightly and suddenly Deadalus and his men were hemmed in against the counter.

Deadalus's stomach tightened and he could feel the sweat on the back of his neck and sides.

"You must be kidding. Certainly you don't mean to say that you think we're in any way connected with this pirate?" he asked with obvious disgust.

"Maybe," the man replied smugly. Deadalus knew that most of the man's boldness was borrowed from the amount of people who stood at his back.

There were a number of different ways in which Deadalus could respond to this affront. He decided to try the calm and logical approach.

"Come now. Didn't you just get through telling me what a fearless and ruthless character this pirate is? Do you really think that this self-appointed king, this sacker of planets, would send me down here to meekly purchase some needed paraphenalia? If he is who you say he is, wouldn't he have just come down here himself and taken whatever he wanted? Can you honestly think that this pirate chieftain would risk a handful of his men by sending them down, unarmed, onto a well-manned and hostile planet merely to buy some food and parts?"

Deadalus looked at them with innocent incredulity.

The crowd shifted uneasily, murmuring among themselves, pointing out the logic in his words. They were well aware that if they were interfering with the freedom of an honest empirical citizen, there would be hell to pay.

"Could be as you say," the troublemaker frowned. "Then again, it could be that you're just down here gathering information before you strike. Or even that your ship is damaged as you say, and you're here to buy the necessary parts and once you've got it fixed you'll be back in full force."

Deadalus looked at the crowd and he could sense their mood changing. The man's words had stirred up their fears and suspicions which had lain just under the surface, ready to erupt.

Deadalus glanced outside. The intuition that something was happening seemed to have spread through the town like the hot wind. The street was filling up with people who stood staring into the small shop.

Deadalus decided that he didn't want to talk about it anymore.

Handing the parts to one of the crewmen, Deadalus was already reaching for his gun when the thick-headed man made a grab for him.

The man stopped as Deadalus pointed the gun in his face. Then, committing the last foolish act of his life, he leaped at Deadalus.

There were some green sparks from the muzzle of the gun and then the man exploded in mid-air like an overinflated balloon.

There was sudden turmoil in the shop. Deadalus, dodging out of the way of the flying pieces of internal organs, led his men through the group of locals who were scrambling over each other in panic.

Outside, the group that had gathered parted readily when Deadalus showed them his weapon. They closed in immediately behind them and someone started shouting for the police. Deadalus decided that it was time to leave.

chapter four

Deadalus was sitting on the bridge of the *Orpheus* when Rhea's landing party finally returned.

Rhea came to the bridge and plopped down wearily in the control seat next to Deadalus's. Deadalus remained silent, waiting for her to speak first.

"We got all the supplies ordered, Captain."

"Any trouble?"

"Not really trouble."

"Then what?"

"A little bit of excitement. Curious, actually. We made good time to Parse, the closer planet. But before we could even land we were commandeered by the police under emergency regulations. We had to take a dozen army officers over to the other planet, Questor." Rhea laughed shortly at the recollection. "I tell you, it sure was something, knowing that any of them would have sold their grandmothers to get our heads, and having them all being so politely grateful for our assistance. I thought it was funny, until I found out why it was they needed our help."

Deadalus stared at her without comment. He felt as if he could almost fill in the rest of the story himself, but he let her continue uninterrupted.

"It seems that a pirate who calls himself Deadalus had just attacked Parse. He and his men overran the police, ransacked the treasury, took what supplies they could get ahold of, and took off before the army could get there."

Rhea paused dramatically, waiting expectantly for Deadalus to react with surprise. She was somewhat disappointed when he regarded her unflinchingly.

"Did you get what we needed on Questor?"

"Yeah. We did manage to finally get everything. Had to argue for it. Fortunately the things we wanted weren't things that Parse needed or we wouldn't have gotten them at all. We had to sneak off too, before they could make up their minds to use our landing craft for more emergency transportation."

"Didn't the army have any ships there?"

"Nothing much. All the cruisers had taken off after this pirate."

"Did they catch up with him?" For the first time in their discussion Deadalus showed some animated interest.

"No, not as far as I heard. In fact they were just going on a hunch. They didn't say what they had to go on but I gathered that it wasn't much. It seems that this pirate has gotten them desperate. Evidently this was the sixth planet in· as many weeks which he had attacked."

Rhea stopped, waiting for Deadalus to comment, but he remained silent, his eyes narrowed in concentration, as if he were trying to see something far away.

"You don't seem very surprised by all of this," she said finally.

"I've already heard about this pirate. We had a little run-in ourselves. Was anyone able to give you a description of him?"

"Sure. A dozen different people. And they gave me a dozen different stories, too. The man that seemed to be in charge of the pirates was this big red-headed man, about six foot four, two hundred pounds, with a deep scar that runs across his left cheek up to his eye. A couple different people agreed on his description, but some people insisted that this wasn't the chief pirate at all, just his second in command. One man who claimed to have seen this pirate Deadalus on a video radio, described him as having a long, thin face, a black goatee, and long black wavy hair slicked back. Some claimed that there really is no one pirate called Deadalus, that it's just a ploy, and that the pirates are really run by a secret group of generals. And then some said that there is a Deadalus, but that he's a crippled genius who never ventures out of his secret hideout. I've no idea which, if any, of the stories I heard was true."

"Any idea how many ships the pirates had?"

"Everyone agreed that the attack on Parse was conducted by two class-B army cruisers. But half the people thought that he has more ships and is able to attack other planets at the same time. The army officers said that they've never had two planets attacked at the same time, and they felt that the two ships was it. But you said that you had heard about this; what did you hear?"

"Not as much as you did. Just some rumors."

Rhea watched Deadalus, waiting for him to continue, but again he seemed to be lost in his own thoughts.

"So what do you think it's all about?"

Deadalus started to answer, hesitated, then shook his head.

"I don't know. It seems too organized and too well planned for the average pirate."

"You think Hissler and the secret police have something to do with it?"

"Possibly. But I just can't figure out what they would gain by it."

"Couldn't they be trying to turn the people against us? Seems that if they make everyone believe that we're a bunch of killers, then we won't be able to find a safe landing anywhere."

Deadalus shook his head.

"I thought of that, but it doesn't hold up. The secret police would have done a much better job at impersonating us. Just using the name of Deadalus obviously isn't enough. Both of us just landed on planets which were up in arms against this pirate, and we escaped identification. They became suspicious of my group, but for no real reason. They would have jumped on anyone who came along just then. None of the different descriptions of this Deadalus fits me, nor are the ships similar. If the Secret Police was behind it, wouldn't they have at least used a starship?"

Rhea was forced to agree. "But then do you think that the use of the name of Deadalus is just a coincidence?"

"I'm afraid I find that too a bit difficult to believe."

"Then what?" Rhea asked, exasperated by Deadalus's inability to come up with an easy, logical answer.

Deadalus shrugged.

Rhea studied the strong features of Deadalus's face. Though free from any expression Rhea knew him well enough to guess at some of the emotions that Deadalus was feeling.

"I suppose you're going to try and do something."

Deadalus smiled.

"Even though it could very well be some kind of trap?"

Deadalus shook his head, still smiling. "Especially if it's some kind of trap."

"And what do you expect to do? This guy's got half of the Empirical army on his tail, and they can't catch him. You think you're going to do any better with just one starship?"

"I'm not planning to use the starship."

Rhea looked surprised. "Oh. Of course not. How silly of me. You won't need any more than a small landing craft to capture them."

"I was thinking more like a lifeboat. And I wasn't planning on capturing them."

"Oh?"

"I thought maybe they could capture me."

Rhea stared blankly at him.

"Oh. Of course. That would be much simpler."

chapter five

For two days Deadalus monitored all the communication channels. He followed the reports from the army ships as they chased after the pirates. It was soon evident that they had lost the trail and were merely wandering around, trying to look busy, hoping for some kind of lucky break. He listened in on the reports being sent to the Governor of the sector, as well as the private reports being sent to the commanding general. From the abundance of information, Deadalus was able to determine exactly how much the army knew, and what precisely their plans were.

Deadalus learned the names and locations of all the planets that had recently fallen prey to the pirates. He ran the information through the computer and came up with a list of a dozen other planets in the sector which fit the pattern. He had too little information though to be able to predict which if any of the dozen planets would be the next attacked.

Deadalus was at first puzzled at how the pirates were so consistently able to get away after the attack before the army was able to get there. He went over and over the reports trying to find some hint of how the pirates did it. Finally he realized that no reports had been received until after the attacks were over and the pirates had already left. Since some of the attacks lasted a day or more this was extremely peculiar. In many cases if the army had received word when the attack started, they could have easily come to the planets' aid before the pirates would have had a chance to get away.

Deadalus realized that the pirates must have some method of completely blacking out the planets' communication, something which was beyond even the secret police's capability. It was hard to believe, but it was the only explanation which fit the facts. The abilities offered to the unscrupulous owner of such a device were immense. Deadalus felt a begrudging admiration for whoever this pirate was.

But for Deadalus's purposes there was an easy solution to the problem this imposed. The planets of the type which were being attacked were of a relatively high technological development and, being such, were usually very noisy across a wide band of broadcast frequencies. Deadalus had only to monitor as many of the susceptible planets as he could, and if one of them suddenly went silent, chances were it was being attacked. Two days later his idea paid off.

"What makes you think they'll come this way?" Whiskey asked, guiding the landing craft in the direction Deadalus indicated.

"Just a hunch." Deadalus didn't elaborate, not wanting to admit to how much of a hunch it really was. He was simply guessing that the pirates would head in the opposite direction from which the army would be coming. It was a long shot, but Deadalus couldn't see any other likely alternative.

"All right, Whiskey. This should be close enough."

Deadalus climbed into the tiny life boat while Whiskey slowed the landing craft down to a standstill.

The life boat was about the size of a large coffin. With the utmost economy of space it provided the basic necessities to keep a single person alive for three months: food, oxygen, water, and hallucinagenics. The hallucinagenics were needed to keep anyone unfortunate enough to be stuck in a life boat for three months from going insane.

Deadalus checked over the controls, what few of them there were. There was two small jets, one on either side, which provided for a minimum amount of controlled movement. The rest of the instruments were given over to numerous devices for calling for help.

Everything functioned and Deadalus sealed himself in.

"OK, Whiskey."

"You sure you've got everything you need?"

"Yes. I'm ready for ejection."

"Are you positive you don't want some stronger firepower? That one little laser won't do you much good."

Deadalus smiled at Whiskey's concern.

"I don't plan to fight with them."

"And you won't have any trouble contacting the *Orpheus* if something goes wrong? I mean what if they pull something fancy and we can't track you?"

"Everything's taken care of. Quit stalling now and eject me."

Deadalus felt the thrust as the life boat was shot out of the landing craft.

Deadalus knew that his plan appeared riskier than it really was. He was going to radio the pirates for help, hoping to intrigue them enough with the promise of payment to convince them to pick up the life boat. Once on board the pirate ship he'd tell them that he had just absconded with someone's money and would ask to join up with them. He was sure that they would be enough in need of volunteers that they wouldn't kill him outright. They would of course be suspicious, but the audacity of the plan would be its own protection.

The *Orpheus*, which was nearly repaired, would be tracking them. Deadalus figured he'd have plenty of time to talk to the leader of the pirates and find out what was going on before the *Orpheus* came and got him. To Deadalus the risk seemed very small and didn't bother him in the least. What did bother him was why he was troubling himself with the pirates at all.

He settled down for what he hoped would not be too long of a wait.

The radio, tuned to monitor the blacked-out planet, hissed with static and the tiny craft was filled with a smell like that of melting tar as the long unused wires grew hot. Deadalus knelt in the small space and, in the flickering lights from the control panel, checked the box stored at his feet. The rectangular metal box was filled with strips of refined silver. Weighing about fifteen pounds, it represented a fortune large enough to interest even the haughtiest of pirates.

After eight hours Deadalus's mouth began to taste funny as the fresh air was steadily replaced by regenerated air. The regenerated air had a slightly different gas content than normal air and, in the close confines of the ship, gave him the feeling of suffocation. Deadalus switched on the small view screen to try and take his mind off it.

To the left was the Omega nebula, a huge cloud of gas turned green by the star at its core. The cloud, when viwed in astronomical terms, was one moment in the birth of a star. It was the gestation period from which, after immense heaves and contractions, a brand new star would emerge. But that was in terms of time far beyond the experiences of man. To Deadalus's eye the nebula was motionless and had been so ever since his ancestors had first hunched out of their caves and looked at the sky.

In the twelfth hour the life boat's detection system picked up a ship approaching. It was a large, slow-moving luxury liner. Cruisers to the out-lying provinces were not all that uncommon despite the fact that there were no real attractions for the exclusively wealthy clientele who patronized liners. Most of the people on the luxury liners didn't care where or if ever they docked. The appeal of the trip was the ship itself, equipped as it was with the maximum of drugs, drinks, and every modern method of debauchery.

In the extremely cramped quarters of the lifeboat, Deadalus watched the passing liner with a bit of cynical envy. The liner passed out of range, and Deadalus was again alone. And he waited.

After another five hours he decided that he might as well go to sleep. He left the radio volume on loud so that any broadcast would be certain to wake him, and he composed himself as comfortably as the circumstances would allow.

"Can anyone out there hear us? We need help! Can you hear me? This is an emergency!"

Startled from the depths of a bad dream, Deadalus made a confused motion as if trying to run and then remembered where he was.

He turned the screaming radio down to a bearable level and scanned the area for the pirate ships. The laser picked them up and Deadalus anxiously plotted the course of their flight.

The ships, as he'd hoped, were coming in his direction, but the angle of their flight was farther away than he liked. Deadalus figured that the closer he was to them the better his chances of getting them to pick him up.

Quickly he pointed the small life boat on an intercepting path and excelerated to the maximum speed that its small jets would allow. If the pirates were going at full speed they'd reach him in less than fifteen minutes.

A half hour later the two pirate cruisers were just coming into range. Deadalus was amazed that they were so sure of themselves that they weren't even hurrying. Using the extra time to his own benefit, Deadalus got his life boat directly in the path of the oncoming ships.

Deadalus flipped on the automatic emergency signals, an array of broadcast signals which were designed to cause the life boat to light up like a christmas tree on the detection board of any nearby ships.

"This is life boat L-seventeen, please help me. I repeat, this is a life boat in need of help, please respond." Deadalus put as much desperation into his voice as he could.

The pirate ships sped toward him, seemingly ignoring his call for help.

"Come on, you guys, you've got to pick me up! I'm going to die in here if you don't! This is life boat L-seventeen, please respond!"

Silently the ships pierced through the blackness, now nearly abreast of him. Deadalus watched them for a moment and then played his trump card.

"Listen, I've got money! I'll be happy to reimburse you for your trouble. I'm going crazy in here! I'll pay you good!"

There was a buzz, then a half-amused gruff voice responded.

"How much?"

Deadalus grinned, but kept the smile out of his voice.

"I'll give you three . . . uh, four ounces silver."

There was a grunt for reply and the ships did not slacken their speed.

"No, wait! I'll give you . . . I'll give you forty ounces! That's all of it though."

Deadalus waited. Forty ounces would not intrigue them, but the way he'd said it might. It would be obvious to them that he had more than he was admitting to.

The closer of the two ships veered toward him, almost imperceptibly slacking its speed.

Deadalus let out a breath of relief. So far so good.

He adjusted the angle of the life boat in preparation of being picked up. To his dismay, the ship bearing down on him gave no indication of slowing down.

"Hey! Aren't you guys going to slow down?"

Deadalus just had time to hear the gruff laugh in reply before the larger ship engulfed his small capsule. There was the sound of tearing steel as Deadalus was thrown against the restraining straps and knocked unconscious.

There was the sound of voices and laughter. The smell of red-hot metal. Deadalus gingerly unbent his neck. The voices vere suddenly drowned out by the teeth-jarring sound of the steel hull being ripped apart. There was a flash of light. Deadalus opened his eyes.

The end of the life boat was smashed in, the thick hull crinkled up like a discarded piece of paper. It was pure luck that he'd survived the impact. Deadalus grimaced. His well-being was evidently not one of their major concerns.

He unstrapped himself, checking his limbs, and to his relief the only injury he'd sustained was a crink in his neck. Everything else seemed to be in working order.

The smell of torched steel grew stronger and then suddenly the laser that was being used to cut the life boat open, pierced through the hull, burning across the panel next to Deadalus's shoulder.

"Hey! Watch out! You damn near cut my arm off!"

Loud laughter greeted his shout. The laser stopped and a face peered down through the crack that had been cut open.

"You missed him, Joe. Try half a foot to the left."

There were some guffaws and Deadalus realized that he couldn't be sure if they were joking. He considered for a moment and then called out pleasantly.

"Hey, Joe!"

The voices outside the life boat fell silent.

"Listen, Joe, I've got my finger on the button for the propellent jets. If you aren't a bit more careful I might get so nervous my hands'll shake. You wouldn't want that now, would you?"

There was some angry muttering as they realized the potency of his threat. The face reappeared in the cut section.

"Take it easy, buddy. You ought to be grateful we picked you up at all."

"That won't do me much good if you cut me to pieces getting me out, now would it?"

"All right. Just hold still. We ain't gonna hurt you."

The face disappeared and the laser came back on slicing a section out of the wrinkled hull. A piece was pulled aside and a hand reached down to help Deadalus out.

Deadalus climbed out and immediately had his arms pinned behind him. He didn't struggle as he was searched for weapons. Looking around he saw that he was in a entry dock usually used for a craft a good deal bigger than his small life boat. The pilot had evidently just opened the bay doors and scooped him up without having to stop.

There were four crew members in the dock with him. Two held his arms while a third searched him. The fourth stood to the side covering him with a weapon.

They found the one gun as he had intended and then stood back.

"Hey, I can't tell you guys how glad I am that you happened by," Deadalus said, smiling and rubbing his arms.

The men looked at him as if suspecting he was either doped up or crazy. The one who had held the weapon walked over.

He was a gigantic man, about six foot eight, and must have weighed over two hundred and fifty pounds. His face could have provided camouflage in a gravel pit, it was so gnarled and misshapened it hardly looked human. The eyes which peered out at him from the crevices of that catastrophe were dull and beastlike.

The man towered over Deadalus for a moment and then raised a ham-sized fist and knocked him down and nearly back into unconsciousness.

Deadalus's head filled with a scarlet, spinning fog and he barely managed to roll out of the path of the man's boot. He rolled again and came up into a crouch, ready to spring at the pirate who slowly advanced toward him.

"That's enough, Dirk. I want him able to talk."

The commanding voice came over the intercom, halting the giant mid-stride.

Dirk growled with disgust but made no further advance.

"Dirk, you and one of the others search the craft. You other two bring him up to the bridge."

By the time Deadalus had been escorted to the bridge, the box of silver had been reported. So far, except for the egg-sized lump on the side of his head, things were going pretty much according to plan. They hadn't killed him outright, which meant that someone was curious enough to want to talk to him. And Deadalus felt certain that he'd get all the information he himself wanted while being questioned.

The captain of the ship fit the description Rhea had given him of the leader of the attackers. He was six three or four, hugely muscled, red hair, and a deep scar across his left cheek. He and Deadalus studied each other. Deadalus was the first to break the silence.

"Ain't it just my luck to get rescued by a pirate ship. I don't suppose you'd consider just putting me back in a life boat and forgetting the whole thing?"

The captain smiled grimly.

"What were you doing in a life boat in the first place? And where did you get all the silver?" The captain's voice was less gruff than his appearance suggested.

Deadalus looked around as if considering his reply, then sighed and sat down in one of the seats.

"I guess it doesn't matter now. No sense in trying to pretend. I sort of removed the silver from its original owners. I had to take off in the life boat so that the police wouldn't sort of remove my head. Rather risky business, but I didn't have much choice at the time."

"Who did you take it from?"

"Why? You planning to return it?"

The captain snorted. "Just curious. Most people don't have that much silver lying about."

Deadalus looked indignant.

"Who said it was just lying around? It took me a lot of work to get that, I'll have you know. You think a heist like that comes easy?"

The captain studied Deadalus for a moment and then, shrugging, motioned for two crewmen to take hold of him.

They dragged Deadalus struggling to his feet.

"Throw him out," the captain said, turning away.

"But it's true! Don't you believe me?"

"Oh, I guess so. Doesn't really matter where you got it. It's ours now."

The two crewmen started to propel Deadalus toward the doorway.

"Can't we make some kind of deal?"

The captain didn't even turn around.

"You've nothing to bargain with, buddy."

"Wait! Let me join up with you. I'm sure you can use me."

The captain laughed, turning around.

"We don't need any more thieves."

"Can you use a pilot?"

The captain looked at him sharply and the two men who were ushering Deadalus out paused.

"Can you pilot?"

Deadalus nodded. He knew that piloting was a rare enough skill that the pirate captain would be interested.

"Why didn't you say so?" The captain motioned for the two men to let go of Deadalus.

The captain had him sit down in the pilot's chair and prove that he knew how to handle the ship. Deadalus asked a few questions and purposely made a few small mistakes, not wanting to demonstrate the full extent of his skill. The pirate captain was satisfied.

"Well, how about it?" Deadalus asked when he was through. He wasn't really concerned whether or not he would actually be accepted as part of the crew. He just wanted to buy himself a little time to find out what he wanted to know, time enough for the *Orpheus* to rescue him.

He looked at the captain hopefully as the big man rubbed his chin in thought.

"Well, you know how to pilot all right. And if it was up to me I'd let you join up with us."

"What do you mean," Deadalus asked carefully. "Aren't you the captain?"

"Yeah. But this kind of decision is up to the

53

boss. And we won't see him for a couple of weeks."

Deadalus tried to cover up his frustration.

"Two weeks! What'll I do till then?"

"Enjoy yourself. It may be your last two weeks alive."

chapter six

Deadalus heard the door lock behind him and looked around. The cabin he'd been put in was ordinary. An eight foot by eight foot cubicle, it contained two acceleration couches, two wall lights, and a closet. Deadalus checked the closet and, finding it empty, sat down to think.

He had two choices. He could have the *Orpheus* come as planned, which would be the simplest thing to do, or he could try and wait until he'd managed to see the pirates' boss. If he let the *Orpheus* come now he would have to accept it as a failure, at least temporarily. There didn't seem to be any way he could get the information he needed without talking directly to the phony Deadalus himself. But if he tried to wait, the *Orpheus* wouldn't be able to track him and he'd have to rely on getting radio contact with them in order to be picked up.

He hated to give up after having come this far; he knew he'd probably never have a second chance. But the additional risk he'd now have to take made him wonder if the information was worth it. What was it that he was after?

Someone was committing atrocities under his name. This of course should bother him, but not to the extent of losing all rational perspective on it. Logically the situation should resolve itself without his intervention. Either the man using his name was merely a pirate, in which case the army would sooner or later catch up and eliminate him, or else it was a trap by the secret police to try and flush Deadalus out. If it was a trap the bait was rather expensive and, if Deadalus just ignored it, they would sooner or later have to drop it.

Yet even as he considered it, he felt his emotions flooding over him. He felt that if he let this pseudo-Deadalus go unchallenged, then he was, in a sense, giving his permission to the foul deeds. Just as Rhea's accusation of self-gain had infuriated him, he felt that this too was unjustly accusing him. He wanted to make a clear distinction between what he did and what this pirate was doing.

But for whose benefit was he making this distinction? For Rhea? For Hissler? For mankind in general?

Or was it in fact just for himself. Wasn't it because deep down he doubted that there was a clear distinction between what he himself did and what his double did? When you got to the point of sacrificing others for your own personal beliefs, did it really matter all that much what those beliefs were? Did it really make any difference if you believed that your end goal was for the benefit of man? Of course

what he himself was doing was obviously not
out of greed. But maybe Rhea was right. How
far could he go without becoming the same as
those he was fighting.

Yet what was the alternative? Was he supposed to let Hissler and the Empirical secret
police go unopposed? Who would benefit from
that? And Deadalus knew better than anyone
that there was no way to fight them other
than the way he was doing it. There was no
way within the system. The only possibility
was by fighting against the system itself.

Deadalus recalled Jay's joke about having
enough to retire on. And it was true. They
could easily divide up the money and go their
separate ways. He could find some small outlying planet where he wasn't known and live out
the rest of his natural life in comfort.

Deadalus shook off the daydream and laughed.
The first thing he had to do was to put a stop
to this phony Deadalus who was ruining his
good name.

He had to contact the *Orpheus* and tell them
to wait. And to do this he'd have to get to a
radio.

The lock on the door provided very little
trouble and Deadalus was soon walking quickly
and cautiously down the corridor. He knew the
layout of a usual army cruiser and, hoping
that this one hadn't been altered drastically,
he headed away from the control room.

If he could get to a radio, it would take him
only a minute to send the *Orpheus* a message.
There was only one transmitter and that was
in the control room, but the computer had ac-

cess to it and so all Deadalus was looking for was one of the computer outlets. There would be an outlet in each of the gun stations, but those were sure to be manned. There would also be an outlet in the engine room and that was where Deadalus was headed.

As he had expected, the engine room was dark and deserted. Except during takeoffs and when there was a breakdown, engine rooms were rarely occupied. The computer outlet was there solely for checking the engines prior to blastoff.

Deadalus quickly found the code number he was looking for. But instead of tying in directly to the radio, he programmed the computer to broadcast his message in ten minutes. That way if by some extreme chance someone did notice the message going out, Deadalus would be back in his room and beyond suspicion. The message was in electronic code and said, simply, "wait."

Deadalus had just left the engine room and started back when he ran into trouble. One of the crew turned the corner into the corridor in front of him. Deadalus immediately turned around and started in the other direction, walking normally to avoid suspicion. It almost worked.

"Hey!"

Deadalus tried to ignore the gruff bark. He was only a few feet from the corner. He took another step.

"Hey damn you!"

Deadalus turned around with what he hoped

was a look of pleasant nonchalance. He needn't have bothered.

The man who had accosted him was the same giant who was responsible for Deadalus's headache.

Deadalus sighed. Out of all the people to have to run into he'd have to chose one of the few men on board who knew him. On the other hand, at least he wouldn't be beset with qualms if he had to break this guy's neck.

"What're you doing?" the man growled, advancing.

"Ah, just the man I was looking for," Deadalus said lightly, watching the other approach. "The captain wants to talk to you."

The man grumbled and made a grab for Deadalus who stepped back smiling, avoiding the other's grasp.

"I was trying to find my way back to my room but I seem to have gotten turned around. If you would be kind enough to point out the direction I'll be on my way."

The man stopped with another small grunt and eyed Deadalus suspiciously.

"I'll make it easy," Deadalus said mockingly. "Just grunt once for yes and twice for no."

It was hard to say whether or not the other's expression changed, but he moved forward, both bucket-sized fists clenched.

Deadalus stepped back, still smiling, but watching warily. The man was wearing a gun but obviously had not thought of using it. Or perhaps he felt so sure of himself that he didn't need it.

The man swung at him and Deadalus dodged

back in time. The wind from his fist felt like a passing train. The man was quicker than Deadalus would have expected, but he was standing flatfooted and was leaving himself wide open.

Deadalus took another step back and was now even with the corner of the hall. He could just take to his heels. That would probably be just as efficient, that is, if this rockheaded fool didn't just shoot him in the back.

A sudden loud siren solved the problem. The pirate hesitated, then, with a low growl turned and stomped off down the corridor.

The ship was alive with movement and Deadalus hustled back to his room, wondering what had caused the call to battle stations and thankful that the grunting giant had been trained well enough to respond immediately to the call.

Deadalus was not kept long in suspense about the battle alert. He had just gotten back to his room and was trying to make up some excuse for having been out wandering around the ship when the cabin door was thrown open.

A crewman stuck his head in.

"Captain wants you on the bridge. Now."

Deadalus started to question, but the man was gone. Whatever was going on, there didn't seem to be much choice but to go and see what awaited him.

The bridge was crowded and noisy and it took Deadalus a moment to locate the captain. He was surprised to see that the men at their stations were smiling and laughing. If there was a battle ensuing it apparently was going to be decidedly one-sided.

Deadalus walked over and stood next to where the captain was seated in the pilot's chair. He quickly took in all the instruments without seeming to do so. The radar showed two objects. The first was the second pirate ship, which Deadalus was glad to see was still keeping a parallel course with the one he was in. The second object Deadalus recognized immediately as a luxury liner, most likely the one that had passed by him earlier.

"What do you think?"

Deadalus looked down at the captain who was eyeing him closely.

"What?"

"I asked you what you think."

The question was obviously calculated and Deadalus felt trapped. If he revealed how fully observant he was the captain could easily become suspicious. Then again, if he played dumb and the captain suspected it, it would arouse the suspicion that he was trying to hide something.

Deadalus saw a half-smile flicker momentarily across the other man's face and realized his moment of hesitation had given him away.

"What do I think? I think that it shouldn't be necessary to use both of your cruisers to board that liner, if that is in fact what you're considering. And, unless your two ships have the unlikely habit of splitting everything evenly, it appears that we are the closer and could easily get there first. But then, I've no idea how you decide such things."

The captain nodded and smiled to himself as if having confirmed something he'd suspected and looked back at the screen.

"You don't think they're heavily armed then?"

Deadalus shrugged.

"Never heard of one that was."

"There's been a lot of trouble in this sector though," the captain's eyes twinkled. "Perhaps they've taken extra precautions."

"You must be extremely undermanned if you're concerned over what feeble defenses a luxury cruiser would have."

The captain bristled.

"I didn't say I was worried. We could take that liner with our eyes closed."

Deadalus looked at him steadily.

"Then why ask me?"

"You said you wanted to join up, didn't you?"

"I said that if the alternative was death, yes, I'd be overjoyed to join with you." Deadalus chose his words carefully, not sure of what was coming.

"Well, you can consider this as part of your initiation."

"How's that?"

"You're going to help us raid that ship."

The captain looked at Deadalus with a hard smile.

"I do hope murder and bloodshed doesn't make you queasy."

Deadalus hid his distaste as the preparations were made. He wanted no part of a pirate raid but could see no way out. He hoped that during the actual boarding everyone would be too occupied to notice if he actively helped or not. He suspected though that the captain fully intended to make certain that Deadalus bloodied his hands, just as proof against Deadalus's being some kind of double agent.

From what he heard Deadalus gathered that raiding the luxury liner was a kind of bonus to the crew, an extra treat that they didn't normally get. The men on the bridge were in high humor, seemingly casual and undisciplined. But Deadalus noted that they all skillfully took care of their assigned tasks. A few of the men looked Deadalus over curiously, but for the most part they ignored him.

Contact was made with the other pirate ship and Deadalus moved in close enough to catch most of the conversation. It seemed that the captain on the other ship didn't think that they should bother with the luxury liner, as it would interfere with a time schedule they had. The reply that the big red-haired captain made sounded as if he agreed, but that he was politically giving in to the desires of his crew. It was arranged for the second ship to go on ahead and wait for them at the next stop.

They closed in on the luxury liner, which appeared at first to just ignore them. Eventually a laconic voice called over the radio asking for their numbers and whether or not they knew they were on a collision course. The pirate ship didn't reply and in a moment the voice from the liner became more concerned. Then the captain of the liner came on and told them to halt or be fired upon. But they had hesitated too long and the pirate ship was too close for them to risk shooting, as it would damage their own ship as well. The pirate captain grinned and finally made radio contact, telling them to stand by for boarding and that any resistance would mean instant death for them all.

The boarding raid was a melee. Like sharks crazed by the scent of blood, the pirates swarmed over the defenseless liner, tearing it to pieces.

At first, the pirate captain had attempted to maintain control over his men. But he had soon realized that they were just too out of hand and wisely stood back, staying out of the way of their mindless destruction.

All of the passengers and crew had been herded into the liner's huge game room and left under guard of half a dozen pirates, while the rest ransacked the ship from stem to stern.

Deadalus stayed with the group in the game room thinking that there woud be less trouble there. He was wrong.

The passengers cowered together like sheep, fearful and uncomprehending. Two of the pirates went among them removing all jewelry and valuables, throwing it onto one of the big game tables. One man hesitated, started to argue and was immediately felled by a blow which cracked open his head, spurting a scarlet geyser of blood onto the plush green carpet. No one else resisted after that.

There was a sudden rush from the other part of the ship. Some shots were heard and then a piercing feminine scream, which rose to an unbearable pitch and then shattered into jagged pieces.

The captain left to investigate and the other pirates glanced at each other, evidently disgruntled at having been left out of the fun. The passengers huddled closer. Deadalus could hear a low sobbing.

The pirates found some liquor and were passing it around when one of the other pirates came in laughing and dumped a bundle on the floor.

"Come and get it while it's still hot, boys," he guffawed.

The bundle turned out to be a girl, no more than fifteen, naked and bleeding from several places. She was evidently the source of the screams they'd heard earlier. The pirate's remark had been more than just a crude jest, as the girl was at the point of death.

To Deadalus's immense disgust one of the pirates took up the offer, and, amid the jeers and catcalls of the other pirates and the screams of the passengers, raped the dying girl.

Bedlam broke loose.

A number of the passengers ran toward the doors and were either shot or clubbed down. The pirates started selecting from among the females and began brutally raping them, killing anyone that offered the least bit of resistance.

The other pirates came back in to join the rampage and, when the captain returned, things were too far gone to stop.

The air was filled with the agonized screams of the assaulted women and the floor was filled with the sticky blood of their husbands and fathers who vainly tried to protect them. Deadalus was sickened by the scene and by his own self-imposed helplessness.

Deadalus started toward a nearby door, hoping to get away from the scene unobserved. He'd only moved a few feet however when a young woman broke away from the pirate who had hold of her and ran in Deadalus's direction.

"Please, please, don't let him get me!"

Deadalus looked up and saw the pirate captain watching him.

The young lady clung to Deadalus's arm as the pirate lumbered toward them, grunting. It was, of course, his old friend lump-face.

Deadalus tried to shake loose from the female's desperate clutch. He already had enough to worry about without getting caught up in the middle of this.

The giant pirate reached him just as Deadalus pulled free.

"Gimme! Mine!"

The pirate slapped Deadalus with one huge paw, knocking him back against the wall.

Deadalus's anger boiled over. He hated having to just stand by and watch, unable to help the people who were being brutally demolished by the pirates and now he had the perfect object to take out his frustrations on.

He moved in and knocked the pirate's hand off the girl.

"This one's mine, cutie. Go find yourself a gargoyle."

The pirate stood still for a moment as if trying to comprehend what was going on. He obviously had not expected Deadalus to put up an argument. With a sudden bellow of rage he leaped at Deadalus.

Ducking under the other's outstretched hands, Deadalus planted a swift kick up between his legs, doubling the big man up and dropping him to his knees.

Deadalus started to move in to put the pirate down for good, but the young lady once again clutched onto him, clinging to him with the strength of a drowning person.

The pirate, his face green with agony, staggered to his feet and drew his gun.

Deadalus kicked the young lady down and dove in the opposite direction just as the man fired. He could feel the heat of the laser as it passed within a hair of his right shoulder.

Deadalus rolled and came up in a crouch. Before he could move farther the captain was there, standing between them, his own gun in hand.

"Put it away, Dirk. Now." The captain's voice was cold and level. It was the voice of a man who didn't plan on repeating himself.

The lump-faced pirate grunted and worked his mouth as if trying to say something.

"We'll finish this properly. Now let's go."

The captain turned and fired his gun over the heads of the rampaging pirates.

"Pack it up," he shouted. "We're leaving."

To Deadalus's amazement the pirates immediately obeyed the captain. They made ready to leave, quickly gathering together the valuables they'd collected.

Deadalus turned to find the captain glaring at him.

"Bring the girl. We'll finish this later."

Seeing no other choice, Deadalus did what he was told and grabbed hold of the young lady who, now suddenly reluctant, tried to run away.

As he followed the others, some of whom were also dragging along female prisoners, Deadalus was uncertain of where he stood. The captain's promise that Dirk could finish it later, properly, did not seem too threatening. Yet Deadalus felt that he had done what was expected. He couldn't see how fighting the big pirate over the girl would compromise his cover.

He'd just have to wait and see. Deadalus shrugged to himself and swatted down the hand of the girl who was trying to scratch his eyes out.

chapter seven

Deadalus finally had to cuff the young lady roughly in order to stop her kicking and biting. He pushed her ahead of him into his cabin and she fell in the corner, sobbing.

On the way back to the ship Deadalus had managed to pick up one piece of contraband and one piece of information.

The contraband he now took out of his tunic, uncorked, and took a long swallow of. Though it was fifty-four percent alcohol, it went down smooth and sweet. A little too smooth and sweet for his taste, but it was the only thing at hand so he didn't fuss.

The piece of information he turned over in his head, happily. He'd overheard two of the crew talking about the sudden departure from the luxury liner. The other ship had been surprised by a local police ship, and damaged. It had gotten away but decided that it had best head back to the hideout. The captain of Deadalus's ship decided that they'd better go along too. This was good news, as it shortened to a matter of days what he had thought was to be weeks.

At the moment though he had an altogether different problem.

The young lady, expecting to be beat, raped, and perhaps killed, was crumbled on the floor, weeping uncontrollably. Deadalus wanted to tell her that she had nothing to fear from him. But to do that he'd have to confide in her, telling her who he really was, and he wasn't about to do that. Deadalus was more concerned with what kind of explanation he was going to give the pirates if they got wind of the fact that he hadn't touched the girl.

He had no idea how long it would be before they found out. It was possible that the girl was considered his for keeps, to do with as he wished. And it was also possible that he was supposed to just use her and dispose of her immediately.

Deadalus walked over to where she was crying and offered her a drink but she was too hysterical to understand or reply. He sat back on his heels, considering.

There was a rap on the door and it was opened. Two crewmen stood in the corridor.

"Let's go, buddy," one of them said, grinning.

Deadalus stood up.

"Where to?"

"You've got yourself a little duel. Dirk's calling you out."

Deadalus took a last swig from the bottle then followed the two of them out, locking the door shut behind him. This was evidently what the captain had meant about finishing it later.

"Is there any way out of this?" Deadalus

asked. "How about if I gave the girl back to him?"

One of the men snorted and the other shook his head.

"Nope.Can't back out of it now. It's a point of honor." He grinned back over his shoulder. "If you're lucky he'll make it quick."

Deadalus wasn't worried about being hurt. The big man was much too slow. What he was worried about was being forced to kill the big pirate. Even in a fair fight it didn't seem like the kind of thing that would make him many friends. It was in fact quite possible that if he killed Dirk the rest of the crew would kill him.

They came to the large eating hall. The tables had been folded up and the crewmen were all standing around the sides, leaving an opening in the center. The murmur of voices paused for a moment when Deadalus entered, but then resumed. On the far side of the room the captain was standing with Dirk. The giant pirate's grin twisted across his scared face like an eel in a coral reef. The voices of the pirates rose and fell as they made and revised their bets, whispering down to a final silence when Deadalus stood in front of Dirk and the captain.

The captain was the first to speak.

"Guess you're going to get more of an initiation than I'd intended. You brought it on yourself, though."

"Is there any way to forego this?" Deadalus asked.

"Afraid not. Once a man calls you out it can't be stopped until one of you is beat."

"You mean I don't have to kill him?" Deadalus smiled.

The captain grinned. "No, you just have to stop him from killing you. It's the same thing. Rather barbaric custom I'm afraid, but it keeps order on the ship."

"Of course." Deadalus turned and looked Dirk up and down, then turned back.

"What are the odds?" he asked.

The captain raised his eyebrows and turned to look at one of the men standing nearby. The man replied with hesitant surprise.

"Uh, fifteen to one. On Dirk."

Deadalus smiled. "Good. Put me down for one bottle of whiskey."

The man looked at the captain, uncertainly.

"A bottle of whiskey? On who?"

Deadalus and the captain both laughed as well as a few of the nearby pirates.

One of the more patient explained to the befuddled pirate.

"If he bet on Dirk, you damn blasted idiot, how the hell could he collect!"

There was widespread laughter now. But it quickly stopped as the captain stepped forward.

"All right. Let's go."

The captain held out long bladed stillettos to Dirk and Deadalus. Dirk took one readily, but Deadalus shook his head.

"Where I come from it's customary to allow the man challenged to choose the weapons."

There was a murmur among the men.

The captain looked at Deadalus narrowly.

"What did you have in mind?"

72

The grin had disappeared from the big pirate's face.

"Oh, I thought we might just use our hands."

The grin returned to Dirk's face and there were disgusted scoffs from the crew. They obviously thought that Deadalus was merely trying to keep from being killed.

The captain regarded him for a moment, then spoke quietly.

"A man killed by a fist is as dead as a man killed by a knife. Use the knives," he advised.

Deadalus smiled and shook his head. The captain was just trying to give Deadalus a chance. A man of Dirk's size was at much less of an advantage with knives than with fists. With a knife Deadalus's faster speed could be perhaps deadly. But with fists the speed really wouldn't matter. That is, with any average fighter.

Deadalus knew that bare hands worked slightly to Dirk's benefit, but he had chosen that in the hope that he might somehow get away with not killing the pirate.

The captain, seeing that Deadalus was set on fighting barehanded, took the knife away from Dirk and stepped back.

Dirk, still grinning idiotically, went into a slight crouch, arms out at shoulder height as if he thought Deadalus planned to wrestle with him.

Deadalus snorted with disgust, turned his back and walked casually out to the center of the room, where he turned and waited for the pirate.

Dirk stared at him in confusion.

Deadalus whistled and beckoned for him as one would call a dog. The spectators, who had been momentarily silent, laughed.

The huge pirate, suddenly aware that the laughter was directed at him, became enraged. He bellowed and charged.

Deadalus leapt spinning, and landed a kick just above Dirk's left ear. The blow would have felled a smaller man, but it merely caused Dirk to stumble and look around as if perplexed.

Deadalus, on the other hand, felt as if he'd just kicked the side of a mountain. Evidently, though it was obviously Dirk's weakest point, the head was not the place to kick him.

Dirk's advance was a bit more cautious this time. Deadalus circled away from him, looking for an opening.

Deadalus's kick to Dirk's head may not have stopped the pirate, but it sure silenced the crew who were watching. As Deadalus circled he could feel the change. It was now apparent to everyone that Deadalus knew what he was doing and that the fight was not going to be as one sided as it had at first seemed.

Seeing an opening Deadalus dove in, striking out at the other's mid-section. He took a blow on his shoulder as he did so, but his own fist nearly doubled up the big man. Deadalus stepped back to get leverage for what would be the final blow, but he suddenly found his arm and shoulder immobilized in a bone-crushing grip.

The big pirate had hold of him. Still gasping for breath, there was nothing Dirk could do yet except hold on, but that was nearly enough.

Deadalus twisted and kicked at the other's legs, trying to knock him off balance, but the pirate merely grunted and swung at Deadalus's head. Though partially blocking the blow, Deadalus still felt as if he'd been hit with a wrecking ball.

Deadalus jabbed, smashing the others adams apple. The pirate's grip loosened and Deadalus twisted away, spun and landed a double-fisted blow to the man's chin.

Dirk tumbled to his knees, clutching at his ruined throat, his face blue.

Deadalus stood back. Except for the heavy rasp of Dirk's struggle for breath the room was silent. He could at this point, kill the large pirate. Everyone could see that. But Deadalus didn't think that it was necessary, as the man was obviously defeated. Even if he could get to his feet, Deadalus could put him down again. Deadalus looked over at the captain.

As he did so, the large man suddenly leapt to his feet. There was some shouts and Deadalus turned. The pirate had a knife in his hand. There were cries of foul. Someone stepped forward to try to break it up but retreated quickly as Dirk slashed at him.

The big man's grin at Deadalus was not a comforting sight. Either he'd been faking the extent of his incapacitation or the pirate was calling on an unheard-of reserve of strength. Either way, the fight was far from over.

The few members of the crew who had taken the odds and bet on Deadalus were causing a fuss. As Dirk approached, circling, there was a brief discussion on the sidelines and then someone slid a knife across the floor in Deadalus's direction.

Deadalus did not take his eyes off Dirk and did not immediately go for the knife. Having been surprised once already by the man's ability, he had no desire to let himself be surprised again.

There was an old rule of gamemanship: when in doubt, assume your opponent's going to make the best possible move. If Deadalus was in Dirk's position, the best move would be to go for Deadalus as Deadalus went for the knife.

Deadalus moved in and let Dirk slash at him, watching to see how the big man moved with the knife. Then Deadalus made as if to dive for the knife on the floor. But at the last moment he stepped beyond it, planted one foot and swung the other in a high arc.

The pirate had done exactly as Deadalus had foreseen, coming down to slash where Deadalus would have been had he stooped for the knife. Deadalus's upswinging foot met the other's downcoming chin. There was a sharp snap and Dirk crashed full length to the floor like a felled tree, his spinal cord severed at the base of his neck.

The room was silent. Deadalus heard someone give a low whistle.

As nonchalantly as he could, Deadalus picked up the knife that was laying between him and the dead pirate and then walked over and took Dirk's knife as well. His every muscle was tense as he half expected to be rushed by the rest of the crew.

There was no movement other than his own.

Deadalus walked over to the captain, unwilling to meet any of the crew's gazes, yet ready to jump into action if need be.

The look on the captain's face was hard to read. It was halfway between admiring appraisal and amusement. The crew seemed to be waiting for the captain to give a sign as to what was to be done.

Deadalus stood a few steps in front of him, unobtrusively holding a knife in each hand. If attacked, he was going to kill the captain first and get his gun. He waited.

A second ticked by in the thick silence.

Finally the captain laughed, stepped forward and slapped Deadalus on the shoulder.

"I think someone owes our pilot here a case of whiskey."

The tension was dispelled. Someone dragged Dirk away to be thrown out and someone else brought the whiskey. The liquor disappeared quickly and another case was brought.

By the time Deadalus returned to his room he'd gained a great deal of respect, a number of friends, and the nickname of Pilot.

All in all things seemed to be working out fairly well and, as he opened his cabin door, Deadalus was looking forward to some long needed sleep.

The sight that met him dispelled any such silly ideas.

chapter eight

Every room in a space ship was equipped with two air ducts, an intake and an exhaust. The intake, usually placed low on the wall, blows a small but steady stream of regenerated air into the room. The exhaust duct, which is commonly placed high on an opposing wall, draws air out of the room at regular intervals, circulating it back to the regenerating chamber. The intake duct is about three inches in diamiter, the exhaust duct, about a foot and a half.

At the moment that Deadalus entered his cabin there was hanging from the exhaust duct the well-proportioned but tightly stuck hind quarters of the young lady he had locked in the room for safe-keeping.

Deadalus swore under his breath. He'd forgotten about her. Sighing, he sat down and regarded the enticing view and tried to think of what to do.

He really didn't want to trouble with her, but he was loathe to hand her over to the pirates. He was too tired right now to try and guard her, but unless he could convince her that he represented no harm, she would probably try to attack him as soon as he fell asleep. But he could not risk revealing to her his true identity. He considered for a moment just leaving her where she was.

He laughed at the idea but stopped suddenly as he heard the sound of her muffled sobbing. She was after all an innocent victim and he had no right to contribute to her distress, regardless of how tired he was.

He stood and took hold of her ankles to pull her out.

She kicked at him violently and he let go.

"Hey!" He banged on the wall next to the duct. "Listen to me, will you? I'm going to pull you out. If you give me any trouble I'll just leave you there and let you suffocate. Understand?"

There was really no possibility of her suffocating, but from her stuck position his threat would seem real.

She stopped kicking and he pulled her carefully out and set her down on her feet.

The expensive evening gown she was wearing had hiked up to her waist and she now pulled it down, straightening the wrinkles and dusting herself off. And then she made a dash for the door.

Deadalus was of half-a-mind to let her go. She managed to reach the door and open it before he pulled her back in.

She bit his hand.

With a yell of surprise he pushed her away. She leapt back at him, trying to gouge his eyes. He grabbed her wrists and she started kicking him.

This was not Deadalus's idea of entertainment.

He got behind her and grabbed her in a bearhug tight enough to cut off her breath. He held her like that for a minute and then eased up, letting her gasp in a lungful of air, then he tightened his grip again. A minute later he could feel the fight go out of her.

He dropped her onto one of the couches. She lay there in a heap, sobbing and gasping. Looking around, Deadalus found the bottle of liquor he'd left and brought it over to offer her a drink. But before he could say a word she was on the floor clinging to his legs.

"Please, please don't hurt me. I'll do anything, just don't hurt me."

Deadalus tried to get her to let go but she clung too tight.

"I'm not going to hurt you. Now come on, get up."

"He'll pay you anything you want," she sobbed as if she hadn't heard him. "Just don't hurt me."

Deadalus finally managed to extricate himself from her grasp.

"Calm down now. I'm not going to hurt you. Just take it easy."

The girl looked up at him, trying to judge his sincerity.

"If you don't hurt me, he'll pay you anything. But if he finds out that ... that something's happened to me he'll kill all of you!"

"Who are you talking about?"

"My father! Commander Ellington!"

Deadalus looked at her with surprise, then sat down on the couch to consider this new information.

Commander Ellington was a high official in the Empirical government and was both rich and powerful. He just might represent the solution to Deadalus's problems of what to do with the girl.

"Commander Ellington, huh? Can you prove he's your father?"

"Of course he's my father. I'm Syndy Ellington. You can ask anyone."

The young lady was quickly regaining her composure as she saw that Deadalus was not making any move to harm her. She stood up, wiping her eyes.

"He wasn't on that cruise with you, was he?"

"No. He's back on Earth. And if he finds out you've hurt me, you'll really be in trouble!"

Deadalus laughed.

"Don't be a fool, Syndy. He can't do anymore than kill us, and that's going to happen anyways, with or without your father. You can't threaten men when they're already condemned. When and if they're caught."

Her face fell as the truth of what he said sank home.

"But . . . but maybe he can pardon you if you're caught?" she suggested.

Deadalus shook his head.

"No chance. Not even your father could pull that many strings."

He offered her the bottle and she took a long gulp. She shuddered and had to clench her teeth to keep the strong liquor down. She sat down and closed her eyes.

"But we may be able to work something out. If you are who you say you are."

She looked at Deadalus with renewed hope.

"Of course I'm me. I'm Syndy Ellington."

"I'm sure there will be some way to prove that. And you think he'd be willing to ransom you back, do you?"

"He'd pay anything!" Syndy was now extremely excited by the possibility Deadalus was offering her.

"He'd be even more generous if you were unhurt, don't you think?" Deadalus asked, leading her to the conclusion he wanted to reach.

"Well, of course." She looked up wondering if he was perhaps teasing her.

"But if you start acting up, if you don't do exactly as you're told, I can't be blamed if you do get hurt, Understand?"

She was instantly on her knees in front of him, pleading.

"I'll do anything you say, I promise. I won't cause any trouble."

Deadalus looked at her seriously, trying to cover his elation at having found such a ready solution to the problem.

"But you'd better understand, Miss Syndy, the rest of the boys aren't likely to care much about our little agreement. And if you get caught alone with them I can't answer for the consequences. And they play pretty rough, as I'm sure you saw."

Syndy nodded, her eyes wide.

"In fact, I'm not certain I'll be able to even

convince the captain to go along with this. So you'd better be on your very best behavior. Understand?"

"I'll do whatever you tell me to. I promise."

Deadalus looked at her sternly, trying to decide just how far he could trust her. Not very far, he knew. But he was willing to risk it.

"All right," he said, pushing the couch into the full recline position. "Right now I'm going to get some sleep, and I suggest you try and do the same. I'll talk to the captain after the next shift and we'll see what can be done with you. And remember, if you try anything—the deal's off."

She assured him adamantly that she would do everything he asked, and, as if to further convince him, lay down on the other couch and strapped herself in.

Her agreement was a little too quick and wholehearted for Deadalus's liking, but he couldn't tell if she was planning something or was simply grasping at what she saw to be her only hope. At the moment though he was willing to take the risk in order to get some sleep.

Even still, he was unable to fall asleep until he was certain that she'd already dozed off. And then it was a very light sleep.

When Deadalus finally awoke and shook the sleep from his head, Syndy was still sound asleep. She was curled up on her side, as innocent and helpless-looking as a child. She was, Deadalus noticed, very pretty.

She had long black hair which fell over her

shoulder and across the smooth skin of her cheek. Her mouth was large, but not inordinately so, and finely shaped. Her nose was small. She had that look, even in sleep, of a spoiled and pampered kid. She couldn't have been more than nineteen.

Deadalus noticed that her straps were undone and he figured that it had just been too uncomfortable for her to sleep, so he left them that way and went to talk to the captain.

"Hey, Pilot. Where you off to?"

Deadalus turned around to see a crewman calling after him. He stopped, waiting for him to catch up.

"I was looking for the captain. Know where he is?"

"Yeah. He's down in the mess hall. Come on, I'll show you the way."

The crewman turned and guided Deadalus back the way he'd come.

"Boy, I've never seen anyone fight the way you do, and I've seen quite a few fights. Where'd you learn to fight like that, Pilot?"

"Back on my home planet," Deadalus improvised. "Ever here of a place called Hesperide?"

The crewman nodded.

"Who hasn't? Pretty rough place, isn't it?"

"The roughest. I used to fly bootleg for one of the pit bosses down there. There was a lot of trouble with the neighboring pits and fighting became a regular part of the job. If you couldn't fight like a maniac and fly like crazy, you were dead. It's funny how much you can learn when your life depends on it."

"Ain't that the truth. How'd you come to leave?"

"Well, the most important part of fighting is to know when not to. One of the other bosses managed to buy out all the police and decided to foreclose on some of his competitors. We didn't have a chance in hell, so I beat it while I could."

"If you can fly like you fight, the boss is sure to make use of you."

"The boss? You mean the captain?"

The crewman shook his head.

"No, the headman. A guy called Deadalus. The captain takes orders just like the rest of us. It's Deadalus who makes all the real decisions."

They were at the door to the messhall now and Deadalus stopped, trying to keep the conversation going.

"The captain said something about that. Who is this Deadalus guy anyways?"

The crewman smiled.

"You'll see."

He slapped Deadalus on the shoulder in a friendly manner and left.

Deadalus stared after him, shaking his head. He hadn't felt like he was being pumped, yet the man had managed to get a lot of information without revealing any. Either he was just a naturally curious fellow, or he was an extremely skilled interrogater.

The thought was driven from Deadalus's mind by the unmistakable odor of frying bacon. Deadalus sniffed and looked around with surprise. He knew he must be mistaken. He'd never heard of a ship carrying fresh meat.

Whatever it was, it sure had his stomach fooled. He suddenly felt ravenous.

Looking across the crowded messhall he could see a long table against the far wall set up with plates of food. He wove his way over, his excitement mounting with each step. Not only was there a huge platter of freshly cooked crisp bacon, but there were a number of cold, smoked hams, strings of still sizzling link sausages, four varieties of ripe, moist melons, bowls of cold fruit, scrambled eggs, hashed potatoes, and a half a dozen pitchers of cold juices.

Deadalus stood staring at the feast, unable to believe his eyes. A crewman came out with a large bowl of a mixed vegetable salad and Deadalus stopped him before he could leave.

"Where is all this food from? How can you possibly have all this on a spaceship?"

The crewman smiled at Deadalus's obvious enthusiasm.

"Just one of the fringe benefits. We got this stuff on our last raid. Have to eat it up or it'll go bad. So help yourself."

Deadalus didn't wait to be asked twice. He got a plate and piled it up with about five pounds of the food. Along with two large glasses of juice, he could barely carry it across the room to where the captain was sitting at one of the tables.

The captain laughed when he saw the piles of food on Deadalus's plate.

"You storing up for the winter, Pilot?"

"I don't often come across this kind of food,

Captain. And I guess I've worked up a little appetite."

The captain chuckled.

"I guess you have, at that. Eat all you want, it'll just end up rotting anyways."

Deadalus busied himself for awhile and when he'd put a sizable dent in the pile of food and somewhat abated his hunger he turned back to the captain who was studying him with amusement.

"Any surprises in store for me today?" Deadalus asked. "Or am I through with my initiation?"

"You're OK by me. And I'll sure put in a good word for you. But like I said, the final decision isn't up to me."

"That's right, you said it was up to this Deadalus character. What's he like?"

"What's he like?" The captain thought a moment. "Well, it's hard to explain. There's nothing I can compare him with; he's just one of a kind. Once you've met him you'll never forget him."

Deadalus ate for a minute in silence.

"You keep talking up this guy, and I can't help but be a little curious about the man who's going to be determining what happens to me. Tell me, how come he's not out here leading you? Seems like he's got it set up pretty good, letting you guys do all the dirty work."

The captain made a face.

"You got it wrong, Pilot. Deadalus is just too valuable to risk himself with these little raids."

"Little? Compared to what?"

"Little compared to the things he's got planned. Right now he's just building up his home base."

The captain didn't describe what these grand plans were and Deadalus didn't want to put him on his guard by asking anything direct. It was likely that the captain wasn't privy to the plans anyway.

"I see, this Deadalus is one of those brainy types who are best off protected from everything."

The captain laughed and slapped his hand against the table.

"Protection! Hah! Deadalus can take care of himself better than any man alive. You did some pretty fancy footwork on Dirk yesterday, but that was nothing compared to some of the stuff I've seen Deadalus do."

The captain leaned back against the wall, taking a long swallow from the glass he held in one huge hand. The room had grown quiet and the rest of the pirates were listening.

"I remember once when we were out in the tri-star sector, you know, the place out near the tip of the third arm? Well, we had just raided a space station that orbits Welsa, a heavy ore planet, and we'd run into all of the worst kink of luck. As we were getting away we came up smack in the middle of a whole army fleet. Deadalus, myself, and four or five others just managed to get away in a landing craft before the ship was demolished. With a lot of tricky flying, Deadalus slipped us right through their fingers, but the landing craft was damaged in the process.

"Deadalus brought us down on a medium-sized satellite of a large gaseous planet in a red giant stellar system. It was a nice-sized satellite, maybe two-third G's, and it had been colonized at some point, though it was long dead by the time we got there.

"The side we landed on always faces the mother planet, and, because of its close orbit, never sees the sun. Most of the lighter atmosphere had of course been stripped away, leaving it cold and dim. What light it did get was filtered through the edges of the mother planet's thick atmosphere and was a deep red in color."

The captain paused in his story, taking a drink, his eyes distant.

"We worked for a couple hours trying to make repairs and then knocked off, calling it a night. Being short handed, we left just a one-man guard. The rest of us fell quickly asleep, tired out by the day's adventures. About halfway through the first shift we were jolted awake by the blood-curdling scream of the guard. I was on my feet, laser ready even before my eyes had finished opening. What I saw made me wonder if maybe I wasn't still dreaming.

"There in the hatch stood this creature which I can only guess was a wild descendant of a genetically engineered grizzly bear. It was over ten feet tall and easily weighed over a thousand pounds. Its fur looked like steel wool and its jaws looked like they belonged on some kind of earth digging machine. This thing stood in the hatch, stooping slightly in order to fit in, and in its front paws it held the limp form of what had been our guard. And as we watched, still too surprised to move, it reached down with those horrendous jaws and popped the head off the man it held like one would pop the cork on a champagne bottle. Half a dozen guns went off at once, as if on arrangement. I tell you, there must have been enough heat on that beast to burn a hole through a mountain. But that didn't stop him, oh no. The beast just reared up, bellowing with rage, and started tearing the place apart. It charged one of the other men, even while he was firing full charge and just sort of reached out and swatted that man like you would some pesky insect. The man was thrown so hard against the wall that I swear we later found an indentation in the hull that was as precisely formed as a picture, it matched his shape right down to his bootlaces.

"We were all still shooting at it and I got a good angle and aimed for its eyes. I'll never know for sure but I think I blinded it, because it suddenly gave a growl of pain and dropped to all fours and started running around in circles as if trying to find its way out. You all know exactly how much room there is in the usual landing craft, and this one was no different. It isn't exactly the place you'd choose to entertain a rampaging ten-foot bear. That monster was bouncing off the walls like some kind of runaway asteroid. The rest of the crew decided that it was a good time to get some fresh air and they all skedaddled out the hatch. I would have joined them myself if I hadn't of backed myself into a corner. I didn't think I could make it to the hatch without getting run over. I had stopped shooting by then, not only was it doing no good, but I was kind of thinking that I didn't want to draw any attention to myself. I looked over at Deadalus, who was standing at the other side of the room. He was just standing there, not firing either, watching that beast with a sort of excited curiosity as if he was playing pinball or something. I was wondering why Deadalus didn't get out, he was right close to the open hatch, when I'll be damned if Deadalus didn't jump right up onto the back of that critter.

"He told me later that he had intended to try and steer the beast out the hatchway, but I didn't believe it then and I still don't. I'd seen that look in his eyes before. He jumped up on the back of that monster just to see if he could ride it and for no other reason."

The captain stopped and took another long drink.

"You asked what kind of man he is. Well, that's the kind of man he is."

The captain looked around as if the story were over. Finally one of the other pirates spoke up.

"But what happened?"

"Happened with what?"

"With the bear! What happened to the bear? Did Deadalus steer it out of the hatch like you said?"

The captain shook his head.

"Oh, no, no. There was no way that anyone was going to steer that thing anywhere. No, Deadalus just hung on for a minute, trying to keep from getting himself smashed as the creature slammed against the walls. The animal didn't pay no more attention to him than if he were a tick or something. Well, after Deadalus had his ride I think he realized that getting back down off that thing was going to be a lot riskier business than getting up had been. So he crawled a little farther up its back until he could reach over and grab ahold of the fur on its forehead. He got a good grip with both hands and then worked up so that his knees were at the base of its neck. Then he just simply yanked back on its head with all his might while pushing down with his knees and snapped its neck. It fell right down dead on the floor."

There were cries of disbelief from all sections of the room.

"Every word of it's true," the captain insisted. "In fact we even ate the thing later when our food ran short."

The captain was about to go on when he was interrupted by a man who had just come in to the mess hall.

"Captain, we got what looks like a dead ship up ahead. You want to come take a look?"

"A dead ship?" The captain stood up. "Come on, Pilot, we'll put you to work."

Up on the bridge the view screen displayed the ship in question. It was a fairly large craft of indistinguishable make and it was stationary a short distance above a small dark planet. On one of the consoles a crewman was attempting to raise the ship, but was getting no response.

Deadalus looked at the ship and the planet and something about it seemed wrong. He went over to one of the small computer consoles and started taking some measurements.

"What do you think Captain?" One of the crewmen asked.

"I don't know. It could be a derelict. Could be abandoned. Can't really tell from this distance."

Deadalus heard someone mutter "ghost ship," and a shudder seemed to pass through the cabin.

They had all heard stories about haunted ships, strange derelicts, which, once you went on, you never came off. Most of the stories were tales told to frighten kids, but some of the old timers adamantly believed them. Deadalus thought that probably somewhere deep down every spaceman half believed the stories.

"We can't tell too much from out here. Why don't we swing closer and see if it looks like there's anything worth salvaging."

Deadalus had just finished the calculations he was making when the crewmen started to carry out the captain's order. They cut the speed and nosed the ship down toward the other craft.

Deadalus looked at the results of his calculations then spun around.

"It's a trap!"

Deadalus's observations was punctuated by the sight on the screen of two army cruisers bursting out from behind the rim of the small planet and heading toward them at full speed.

chapter nine

The captain looked with surprise from Deadalus to the view screen and back again.

"Full reverse thrusters," he said over his shoulder, moving quickly and hitting the call to battle station's siren.

Deadalus stood motionless in indecision. The captain had just given the wrong order, he was falling for the trap and they'd for sure be caught by the army cruisers if they followed his course of action. And Deadalus had no desire to become one of Chief Hissler's guests. But could he risk arguing with the captain and trying to countermand his order?

As the crewman started to put on the reverse thrusters Deadalus realized he had no choice and sprung into action.

"Excuse me, Captain," he said, bruskly shouldering the man aside and getting into the pilot's chair before the other man knew what was going on.

"Why don't you let me handle this, OK? I am a pilot, remember." Deadalus smiled and strapped himself in, not waiting for the captain to make up his mind. "Cut reverse thrusters," he ordered.

The crewman hesitated, looking at the captain. The captain studied Deadalus for a moment, then looked over at the crewman.

"He's the pilot. Do what he says."

"Maximum speed forward," Deadalus barked, studying the screen.

"Three ships behind us!" someone called out, confirming Deadalus's suspicions.

The forward thrust knocked down anyone who wasn't strapped in. The captain got up and hurried over to a vacant couch and strapped himself down.

The speed of the ship was much greater than Deadalus had imagined. He had heard that the ships had been souped up, but he hadn't imagined anything like this. He grinned. This should be fun.

Two rockets passed close by, aimed at the spot they had been the moment before. The two army cruisers in front of them were taken by surprise. They'd been expecting the pirate ship to try and turn and run, as the captain had in fact started to do. Now the pirate ship was heading directly toward them at an incredible speed.

The foremost of the two army cruisers overshot them and the second tried to desperately to readjust. Deadalus twisted around it, got it dead in the sights, and fired two rockets. Both hit.

The three ships behind had picked up speed and were giving chase. Deadalus turned the ship and dove straight down toward the planet.

At the speed they were going they would crash into it in about ninety seconds.

"What the hell are you doing, pilot?" The captain barked.

"Just hold on tight," Deadalus said evenly.

The gravity of the planet was now added to the ships own force. The hull started vibrating as they reached an enormous speed, far beyond what the ship was designed for. The G-force was so much that it started to over-ride the ship's generators and Deadalus could feel himself being pressed down into the exceleration couch.

Deadalus waited for the very last moment and then pulled the ship out of the dive, parallel to the planet's surface. If the planet had had any kind of atmosphere the maneuver would have instantly fried them to a crisp.

Deadalus fought to keep the ship on course. The ship was nearly flying sideways now as Deadalus struggled to keep the nose pointed in a tight circle, parallel to the small planet's surface. The tail end of the ship kept getting above them almost as if they were in a skid. But Deadalus kept them in line and he didn't slacken the speed even though the ship was now vibrating a lot more than he preferred.

What he was doing was using the small planet's gravity to increase the ship's speed, far beyond anything the ship itself was capable of generating. Pivoting around the planet, he came back around it as if thrown from an ancient sling. So much speed had he picked up from this daring maneuver that he came out directly behind the three army cruisers which had been attempting to catch up with them.

They were going so fast at this point that Deadalus could get off only three shots before the pirate ship had sped out of range, and he wouldn't have gotten even those off had he not been prepared. His first shot missed but the other two went home, bringing down two of the three cruisers. Then the pirate ship was gone, far beyond the reach of the remaining army cruisers even if they had the heart to give chase.

Deadalus relaxed.

"All right, cut the engines."

As the speed abated, the crew on the bridge picked themselves up, shaking out the G-force kinks. The captain came over and checked the display board to make sure that the ship hadn't been damaged in any way, then he turned to Deadalus.

"Mind telling me how you knew it was a trap?"

"As soon as I saw that ship on the screen, it looked out of place that close to the planet, so I had the computer determine the planet's mass and gravity and the dead ship's distance from it and the results showed what I had suspected. The ship was too close to the planet to be in a stationary orbit. It would have been pulled down into the planet within a week's time. It didn't prove anything, but it sure made it suspicious."

The captain nodded appreciatively. "And how did you know that there were going to be ships coming from behind us?"

"That's just the way it's usually done." Deadalus smiled. "You see, it's an old pirate trick, to hide behind a small planet or moon like that. And whenever it's done with more than one ship, they always send the stronger force to come up behind because, as you yourself saw, that's the natural reaction of the prey."

"Yes," the captain smiled unembarrassed. "I guess you saved us a nasty one that time. But that maneuver you pulled, I'm not too sure I'd like you to do that again, regardless of the odds. You damn near shook this old crate to pieces!"

Deadalus was frowning thoughtfully and merely shrugged off the captain's comment.

"Yes, I suppose there was the chance of that."

The captain studied him, taking note of his frown.

"Something bothering you, Pilot?"

"I don't know. Like I said, that's an old pirate trick, but I've never seen it done quite in that manner."

"So? Those weren't pirates doing it either."

"That's just it. They were using a lure."

"And why doesn't that make sense?"

"It makes sense, all right. But there's only one kind of fish you're going to catch with that type of lure."

"Oh," the captain caught hold of what Deadalus was thinking. "It was designed especially for pirates. I see. No one but a pirate would have swung down to investigate a dead ship like that."

Deadalus smiled grimly, only half agreeing. They could have been after pirates, but he thought not. It seemed quite clear to him that the trap had been designed specifically for the starship *Orpheus*.

After things had settled down and they'd called the other ship to tell them what had happened Deadalus managed to pull the captain aside in order to talk to him about the girl, Syndy.

"Now what?" the captain sighed, eyeing Deadalus with a look that said he'd wished he'd never picked him up.

"She's Commander Ellington's daughter."

"So?"

"Well, she was telling me how much her father would pay to . . ."

"We don't do that," the captain said briskly, cutting him off.

"Why not?"

"The boss just doesn't. I don't know why. I didn't ask him."

"I see." Deadalus thought for a moment. "Do you think he might be willing to change his mind?"

"I really doubt it. What's so special about this girl?"

"Nothing. Except she's Ellington's daughter and Ellington's a pretty powerful man. I'm sure he'd pay well. What do you usually do with the females, then?"

"Listen, Pilot, if you're through with the girl I'm sure one of the others would be persuaded to take her off your hands."

"No, no, it's not that. I just thought that the idea of ransom sounded good."

The captain studied Deadalus closely and when he spoke his voice was firm and clear as if he didn't want any chance of being misunderstood.

"Listen to me, Pilot. I like you, you seem like a nice enough guy, so don't get me wrong. But there's obviously more to you than you're telling us. Most of us on this ship have something to hide, I guess. You don't get into this line of business because you're an exemplarary citizen. But there's a lot about you which doesn't match up to the kind of things you've been telling us. You just popping in out of nowhere like you did, and the way you handled Dirk, and then again the way you blasted down three out of five army cruisers when they seemed to have all the advantages. You must admit it's enough to make a guy a bit suspicious. I'm not worrying about it though because I don't have to. You couldn't cause very much trouble here on our own ship even if you wanted to. So I don't have to worry about what to do with you. That'll be up to Deadalus."

"Yes, so you've said."

"So I've said. But I think maybe you've been getting the wrong idea. I wouldn't want you to think that I haven't questioned you closely simply because I believe all the stories you've told me. I haven't bothered trying to find out the truth because I haven't had to. But I would hate for you to go in with the wrong impression of Deadalus. You've got to understand what kind of man he is. He's got some kind of evil power. Don't laugh because I'm not joking. I'm not a man who scares very easy but I'm willing to admit that Deadalus scares the crap out of me. I'm not threatening you, I'm just trying to give you a warning. You had better play it straight with Deadalus because he knows when you're lying. He can tell. And if he doesn't take to you he'd as soon blow off your head as look at you. My advice is to just do what you're told. Don't cause any more waves than you have already. Just play it cool, Pilot, and maybe you'll still be with us next trip out."

Deadalus put his hands in his pockets.

"OK, Captain. And thanks for the advice."

The captain slapped him on the shoulder and then left. Deadalus started down the corridor back toward the mess hall. He'd only gone a few steps when he stopped and patted his sides and pockets.

He'd just realized that he only had one knife. When he went to sleep the night before he'd had two.

chapter ten

Syndy was standing against the far wall when he opened the door and when she saw that it was Deadalus she acted relieved.

"Where have you been? I woke up and you were gone."

Deadalus folded down the utility table out of the wall and set the tray of food down on it.

"Don't tell me you missed me," he smiled.

"I didn't have any idea where you were. What's been going on?"

Deadalus ignored her question for the moment and handed her the bundle he had under his arm.

"I brought you a change of clothes. It's not very elegant, just a ship suit, but it'll be better than trying to live in that evening gown."

She held up the blue jumpsuit skeptically, her small nose wrinkling slightly with distaste.

"Why don't you try the food? I brought a lot, I thought you might be hungry. It's pretty good stuff."

"What happened?" Syndy asked as she sat down and hungrily looked over the food. "I heard a siren, that means an emergency, doesn't it? And then I thought I was going to die, the way we excelerated. Were we attacked?"

Deadalus nodded, watching as she delicately ate a few bites.

"Uh-huh. Ambushed, to be precise."

"Who by?" she asked, unable to hide the quickening of her excitement.

"Army. But don't get your hopes up, we easily outran them. Besides, you'd best understand that you can't expect any help from that quarter. If the boys on this ship did get caught, they'd go down fighting. And everybody on board would go down with them."

She looked down at her food as she ate, for a minute saying nothing.

"Aren't you going to have any? she asked, glancing at him quickly, then looking away.

"I've already eaten."

There was another silence, longer this time. Deadalus studied her, trying to guess what was on her mind.

"Did you talk to the captain? You know, about calling my father?"

"Yeah."

"And what did he say?"

"It's not up to him. A decision like that has to be made by the top guy, a man called Deadalus."

"Is this Deadalus character on the ship? Why can't we go ask him?"

"No, he's not on board, unfortunately for both of us. Seems he's back at wherever it is the pirates use for a hide out. That's where we're headed now. We'll be there within a day or so, from what I gather."

"Do you think there'll be any problem? I mean, won't he want to ransom me?" Her voice was so low that Deadalus had to lean forward to hear her even though he was sitting only two feet away.

"I really can't say, Syndy. But let's not worry about it until the time comes. It's a waste of energy to worry about things which are out of your control."

The young lady had stopped eating. She sat staring down at her hands clenched tightly in her lap.

Deadalus reached over and touched her knee gently. She started back violently, pulling her legs aside. Then quickly looked up at him, frightened.

"I'm ... I'm sorry. I'm just upset. Please don't get mad."

Deadalus smiled.

"That's all right. Quite understandable considering your situation."

She looked at him curiously.

"You certainly aren't what I expected a pirate to be like."

"To tell the truth Syndy, I'm not really a pirate. At least, not yet. I'm brand new around here. I ran into this bunch by accident just before they raided your ship."

Her mouth turned down skeptically.

"You certainly seem to have embraced their cause rather quickly."

"It was either that or be chucked out the

waste chute, which isn't a very exciting prospect in deep space. Yeah, I embraced their cause as quick as I could. But my standing around here is still only tentative. You see, the captain here can't let me join up until I've been OKed by this Deadalus. So we're both in the same bind."

"Would you escape if you had the chance?"

"That's hard to say." Deadalus studied a moment. The question bothered him somehow, he wasn't certain why. Something about it being too apt.

"If it was a real good chance, I probably would. There are certainly a lot of other places I'd rather be. Then again, it's not exactly to my disadvantage to be here."

Deadalus then told her a slightly altered version of the tale he'd told the pirates when they'd picked him up. He kept the general facts consistent, he was in too tight a spot to try and carry off two different stories. But he slanted it slightly, not wanting to put himself in too ugly a light. The very things that would ingrate him with the pirates would alienate him from the girl.

She frowned, puzzled, after he had finished.

"I don't understand. Why then, did you defend me back during the raid? I mean, wouldn't it have been better for you to stay out of it?"

"Maybe." Deadalus smiled. "Perhaps I just don't have the right instincts for a pirate. I can't help but come to the rescue of a pretty young lady in distress."

Syndy looked away from him, smiling.

"I hope it didn't get you in too much trouble."

"Depends on how you look at it."

"What do you mean?"

"Well, after we got back here the pirate I took you away from, a prehistoric fellow named Dirk, decided to call me out."

"You mean a duel? What happened?"

"Since I'm the one telling you the story, the answer to that should be obvious."

She looked amused for a brief moment then her expression changed to horror.

"You mean . . . you mean . . ." she couldn't finish the sentence.

"I assure you that it was no great loss to mankind. In fact it's questionable whether or not he ever was a member of the homosapien species."

Syndy shuddered.

"I hope you didn't get in too much trouble. I don't know where I'd be without you."

Deadalus met her earnest gaze with a smile. Syndy looked down modestly and finished eating. Deadalus noted that despite everything, the young lady had a good appetite.

When she was through she pushed the plate away and carefully wiped her hands.

"What will happen to me if I'm not ransomed?"

"I don't know."

"Could you find out?"

"I asked once and they didn't give me an answer. I'm not going to make a pest of myself about it. There's a number of other female prisoners. I can't say for certain, but I don't think they'd be dragging all of you along just to kill you. If that was their intention they would have done so already."

"Yes, there seems to be some purpose. But what can it be? From what I've heard of this Deadalus character, it's bound to be something complicated."

"Oh? What have you heard?"

"There have been stories going around for a while about a pirate named Deadalus. Some say that he was a renegade from the secret police and that he goes around pretending to help the poor while making himself wealthy."

"How does that fit in with all this?"

"Who knows? Maybe he's gone crazy. Maybe he plans to take over the galaxy."

"I guess we'll find out soon enough."

"Yeah." She shook her head despondently. "If we're still alive."

"Hey, don't talk that way. I'm not going to let them hurt you, kid. I promise."

She smiled. "I'm not a kid."

"Oh, you aren't, are you? How old are you?"

"I'm eighteen and I've done more than you could imagine."

Deadalus laughed. "I doubt that. I've got a pretty vivid imagination.

Syndy gave him a look which made him realize that whatever else she had done in her eighteen years as a rich man's daughter, seducing men was definitely one of them.

Deadalus thought he'd better change the subject.

"By the way, I want my knife back.'

"What knife?"

"The knife you took when I was sleeping."

"I didn't take any knife. Honest!" Syndy sounded sincerely puzzled and for a moment Deadalus wondered if perhaps he'd guessed wrong. She was a better actress than he'd suspected.

"If you don't believe me, why don't you search me?" she offered in a low voice, standing up.

Deadalus grinned.

"If I have to take it away from you, I will. But it would be a lot easier for both of us if you just give it to me."

She studied him.

"I want to keep it," she said finally. "I feel safer with it. What if one of the other pirates came in while you were out? I'd have to have something to protect myself with!"

"You'd probably just get hurt worse if you tried to pull a knife on one of these guys. You probably don't know the first thing about using one."

"Quite the contrary! I know enough to give any of these slobs a second thought!"

Deadalus looked her over thoughtfully.

"If you're that good with one, how can I feel safe? I won't be able to turn my back on you."

"Don't be silly. I took it from you while you were sleeping. If I was going to try anything, that would have been the perfect time, wouldn't it?"

Deadalus considered. It probably wouldn't be that bad of an idea to let her keep it. He was pretty sure she felt that he was on her side, that she would gain absolutely nothing by turning on him. And if she could use it like she said, it just might come in handy.

"Come on," she pleaded. "I've got to have some kind of weapon."

"All right. But don't pull it unless you absolutely have to." He sighed. "Your father must have very peculiar ideas on how to raise a daughter."

Syndy came over and put her arms on his shoulders, looking up into his strong face.

"My father isn't always around. And even a rich girl has to defend herself."

Deadalus smiled down at her.

"Let's not add any more complications to an already complicated affair," he offered.

She smiled and stepped back. But only to undue the snap on her gown, dropping it to the floor.

She was right. She wasn't a kid.

She stood in a light blue one-piece outfit that was designed from the viewer's standpoint. It was all lace and suggestion and what it suggested was more than Deadalus had imagined. It made all sorts of promises, and Syndy's well-developed body kept every one of them.

Deadalus shook his head. He was not going to take advantage of the young lady. Not after having gone to so much trouble to keep her out of trouble.

She looked at him, her mouth open in astonishment. She had probably never had such an offer turned down before. Not with the persuasive argument her body gave.

"You'd better put on that jump suit I gave you, young lady."

"Oh, come on. We've got to do something until we get to their hide out. Why not enjoy ourselves?"

"I plan to," Deadalus smiled and pulled from his pocket a deck of playing cards. "Get dressed and I'll teach you something really exciting."

chapter eleven

A space ship is a delicate creature and, during flight through deep space, even the newest, most sophisticated ships need to be constantly monitored. An older ship, such as the cruisers the pirates were using, needed more than just monitoring. They needed to be forever coaxed, pampered, jimmied, and tricked into sustaining under the incredible demands of deep space flight. To provide this constant care, the crew was divided into three groups, each of which worked an eight-hour shift.

It was at the beginning of the fourth shift after the ambush when the pirate ships came in sight of their homebase. Deadalus had just come on duty, relieving the captain as pilot. The captain stayed on the bridge though to oversee the landing.

As far as Deadalus could tell the planet was not on any current charts, though he was certain that it must have been, a long time ago.

"What's her name?" Deadalus asked the captain, who was standing next to him watching the planet loom ever larger in their display screen.

"The boss calls it Newearth. But most of the boys just call it home."

"What's the story on it? Was it ever colonized?"

"Yeah, it was one of the earliest to be developed. It's a prime size, point nine three G's, and it's a good distance from its mother star, just enough to maintain a long-lasting and dynamic atmosphere."

"What happened? The dark ages get it?" Deadalus asked, referring to that enormous black space in galactical history when the empire structure collapsed and all the worlds turned in on themselves.

"No, kind of funny, actually. Funny or sad, depending on how you look at it. Seems that it was getting through the dark ages with very little problem. It kept a great deal of its technology, and even developed some new stuff of its own. And the planet itself is one of the most fertile planets I've ever seen. You can grow any plant you want here. And there also seems to have been an abundant supply of heavy ores. Not enough to go conquesting off into space of course, but certainly enough to maintain a high level of productive technology. They seemed to have it all set up to make it through those times without any problem. But then I guess they just ran short of common sense."

"How so?"

"They simply killed the planet by overdevelopment. They let the population get out of hand even though they had all the necessary know-how for population control. They over-farmed, overminded, and overbuilt. The cities died from simply having too many people in too small a place. The people spread out, killing the land by their sheer mass. The ground could no longer recycle itself. It couldn't purify the water fast enough. The poisons in the soil and water built up to a critical point where the people ended up poisoning themselves to death. And they nearly killed the planet with them. It's only now starting to get back into shape. The majority of the land is still too contaminated to live on."

They circled the planet, using it to slow them down and then the captain told Deadalus to follow the other ship in. They passed over the ruins of a few cities and then landed a few miles from one of them, on a hard-packed dirt field.

The building that they had landed near was a huge, castle-like structure with a river on one side and a jungle creeping in on the other. The men poured out of both ships, mingling together noisily until the captains called them to order and assigned them tasks.

Syndy and all the other women prisoners on the ship were herded onto a large-transport hovercraft and taken away toward the castle. Deadalus joined in with most of the others in unloading the cargo into transport crafts to be taken to the storehouse.

The temperature was much colder than Deadalus would have imagined from the clear sunny sky. He asked one of the other men about it and was told that Newearth was only cold for a couple months out of the year. The other seasons varied from heavy rain, to gale winds, to summer heat, and finally to a mild, pleasant spring. The weather would not change for month long stretches, and then would change suddenly and readily. He was told that it really wasn't as bad as it sounded because for the first week or so of the new weather it was always a relief over whatever had been before. And by the time you started getting tired of what ever it was, it was time for another change.

When the transport vehicles were all loaded and driving back in a line to the fortress, Deadalus saw a group of men come out from the edge of the jungle carrying large, bulky bundles strapped to their backs. Deadalus pointed them out to the driver and asked about them.

"That there's a monkey party."

"A monkey party? What's that?"

"It's a hunting party. Started out as just a way to relieve some of the boredom, something fun to do. But now the boss has got them organized, bringing in meat and hides."

"What do they hunt?"

"Monkeys mostly. The entire planet's infested with these primates. They're real pests. They'll steal anything they can get their hands on, from food right up to a hovercraft. And they're dangerous too. If they catch you alone in the jungle you're done for."

Deadalus looked at the band of hunters as they drove by them.

"Do you always hunt them on foot like that?"

"Have to. There's no other way to do it. You can't take a hovercraft five feet into that jungle there. So unless you want to go and try to pick them off out in the ruins, you have to go on foot."

"The ruins? You mean that city we flew over coming in?"

"Yeah, for some reason they hang around there a lot. But it's as hard to get them there as in the jungle. There pretty damn smart for monkeys. Makes for a good sport, it does. And of course there's the hides and meat."

"The meat I can understand, you can always use meat. But what do you need the hides for?" Deadalus asked, puzzled.

The man opened the lapel of his coat to show Deadalus the fur-lined underside. Deadalus could now see that the whole coat was made of hides stitched together with the skin side out.

"As soft as mink and as durable as leather. Waterproof too."

Deadalus had a lot of other questions in mind but forgot them as they drove through the fortress-like walls. The building was the size of two city blocks and was three or four stories high. The vehicles drove down a tunnel that led under the structure and what struck Deadalus was how old the place was. The stones that supported the building looked to be thousands of years old. Age hung on them like cobwebs and dust. That a building that big could still be standing after so many eons was a tribute to the builder's engineering.

The transport vehicles came to a stop in a

large storage area and started unloading. The pirates stacked and recorded all the various treasures they had stolen in as mundane and business-like manner as if they were all public accountants. To see such discipline in men who were by nature so uncontrollable once again brought to mind the power of the man who led them. Deadalus helped, doing what was assigned him, wondering how long it would be before he'd have his confrontation with the pirate boss.

When they'd nearly finished the unloading, a man wearing a green silk armband came up to Deadalus.

"Are you the new man" he asked, looking at Deadalus and checking a list he carried.

Deadalus nodded.

"All right. Follow me."

The man turned without further explanation and started across the storage area. Deadalus wiped his hands on his pants and followed, feeling a sudden excitement tumble in his stomach.

"Where are we off to?" he asked, but the man with the silk armband didn't answer.

Deadalus followed the man up a long, narrow stairway, down a hallway, around one corner and another, up another stairwell and down another long hallway.

They passed room after room. Some with closed, heavy stone doors, some with no doors at all. Everything he saw gave Deadalus the feeling of strength and durability, age and history. He was fascinated and would have liked to stop and look over many of the things he saw, but he had to hurry to keep up with the man who was leading him. Deadalus settled in to memorizing the path they were taking.

Finally, down another narrow hallway, the man came to a stop in front of one of the closed stone doors. There was a number scrawled in chalk on the jamb and the man checked it against the list he held.

"Seven fifty five. All right, this is it. This and everything in it, is your room. I advise you to write the number down and carry it with you because you're bound to get lost a dozen or so times in the next couple of days."

The man turned on his heel and left before Deadalus had the chance to ask him anything. Deadalus watched his back until he turned out of sight around a corner, and then he looked at the door.

He had hoped that he was being taken to the boss. He was getting tired of this continual waiting. It seemed to be just one postponement after another. Maybe the rumors about there being no real boss were true. Maybe Deadalus was just a fabricated name used for a group of men. Maybe he'd never come face to face with the leader, or, if he did actually see someone, maybe he would be as phony as everything else.

Deadalus sighed with disgust and opened the door. Every step he took seemed to mire him deeper and deeper until he had the feeling that he could never turn around and leave.

There was someone standing across the room next to the deep window. She turned around and glared at him as he opened the door. She had long black heavy hair pulled back into half a dozen braids, her features were sharp and distinct, with high cheek bones, straight nose, and large sensual mouth. Her eyes were large and almond shaped and from where Deadalus was standing he was unable to see what color they were. But the emotion they were alight with was quite clear even from this distance. She was furious. It was the type of anger that could come from only great pride and self-confidence. It was not a cringing, submissive sort of anger.

Deadalus smiled.

"Hello. Do you come with the room?"

For a moment he thought she was going to spit at him, but then she just turned away and looked back out the window. Leaving the door open, Deadalus crossed the room, studying her as he did. She was long and hard, with the lines of a first class racing horse. Almost as tall as himself, the muscles of her arms and legs looked strong and well used. The skin that showed on her long neck beneath her braids was dark. Deadalus came to a stop on the other side of the window and looked out.

And stared.

It wasn't a window at all, bur rather an observation hole that looked into a huge aquarium. Lit from some unseen source, the water was dark turquoise, filled with vague shadowy shapes that moved and swayed as if to music. A large, peculiarly ugly fish swam by, rubbing its thick, encrusted stomach against the glass.

Deadalus involuntarily stepped back and

looked over at the lady. A small smile was now playing around the corners of her mouth.

"Excuse me but I'm new here and I don't really know what's going on. It would be nice if you told me who you were and what you're doing here and why you're angry with me."

She looked out the window into the deep blue water for a minute without answering. When she did finally speak, her voice was low and had the sound of woodwinds.

"My name is Clea and why I'm angry is none of your goddamn business."

Deadalus rubbed his chin thoughtfully. This being a pirate was evidently not the way to win lady friends. The woman looked interesting and intelligent and Deadalus could really use someone to ask questions of right now. But it was obvious that being polite was not going to get her to open up.

"Well, if that's the way you're going to be," he said finally, "you'd best just get out."

She looked at him quizically.

"What?"

"I was told this was my room. Now if you won't tell me what you're doing here, you can just leave."

She threw her head back and laughed, displaying one of the prettiest throats Deadalus had ever seen.

"I come with the room," she said, her voice still angry. "I'm assigned to you. Just like the bed. I'm your breeding partner."

It was Deadalus's turn to be taken aback.

"My *what*?"

"We all must do our share for the good of the whole. Didn't they tell you?"

"No, they didn't tell me. Why do you think I was asking you? I don't know what's going on at all. They just brought me here and told me this was my room. If you'd care to explain how things work around here I'd be much obliged. You act like I've done something to you but I've never even seen you before." He glared at her, returning her anger ounce for ounce.

"They really did pick you up in the middle of space, didn't they?"

"Who told you that?"

"Oh, I've heard." She turned away. "Word gets around pretty fast."

"What else have you heard?"

She turned to him with a smile.

"I've heard that you ask too many questions."

She looked as if she was about to say something more, but then turned and walked back across the room. Deadalus's eyes followed her.

She was wearing a light tan ship's suit which had been altered into a much more feminine outfit. The sleeves had been cut short and cuffed and the legs had been cut off above the calves and held in place by a band of elastic. A number of darts had been put in to make the waist and bodice better fitting. There was also some delicate, dark brown flowers embroidered along the collar and down the front right side of the zipper.

She stood at the door as if momentarily undecided, then pushed it shut. She turned around and looked at him carefully.

"This is the way it goes. Each man is given

a female. The woman is charged with cleaning up after him so that this place is kept from degenerating into the trash heap it would become otherwise. The female also serves as a handy object to drain off the man's excessive high spirits by allowing him to beat up on her and fornicate with her whenever he feels like it. This manages to keep a general peace among these cutthroats who would otherwise be cutting each other's throats. Thirdly, these assigned females are to serve as breeding partners. The high and holy Deadalus has somehow got it into his head that it would be fun to fill this planet with another generation of little bastards. So you must forgive me if I'm not just absolutely tickled with my lot in life. As far as I know you don't have a choice in the matter any more than I do. I don't think he'll let you change the assigned female, though it might be interesting to watch you try."

She said all this in a straightforward manner while watching him with a sort of amused curiosity.

Deadalus smiled. "You change moods faster than anyone I've ever met," he said appreciatively.

Clea considered the comment and appreciation and then shrugged.

"What do you want me to call you?" she asked.

"Oh, I'm sure you'll think of something."

Deadalus turned his attention for the moment to the details of the room.

Everything was made out of what appeared to be a gray natural stone, cut into even, smooth blocks three feet high by three feet wide. Judging by the depth of the window, the walls were about two feet thick. Over in one corner was a thin slab projecting from the wall to serve as a sort of table. Next to it were two stools of a thin plastic obviously not native to the building. The main part of the room was taken up by the bed which Deadalus at first feared was made from another block of stone. But when he went over and pushed down on the blankets he was relieved to find it soft and giving. Evidently a large hollow had been scooped out of the stone and filled with some suitable material.

On the far wall was a thin doorway which turned out to lead into a fairly large bathroom or dressing room. There was a closet and a metal mirror, and the entire back half of the room was taken up by a giant, sunken tub. Along the walls in both rooms were lanterns which appeared to use some sort of liquid fuel.

Clea was still watching him after he had finishd his brief inspection.

"If you know how they found me then you should know that I'm no happier with this situation then you yourself are. You sound as if you've been here a while."

Clea looked away from him and didn't answer.

"Were you given special instructions not to answer my questions?" he asked, moving over so that he stood directly in front of her.

She met his gaze. There was no sign of fear or submission in her look.

"I've been here nearly two years."

"Oh? And what became of your last, uh, breeding partner, as you say."

Her answer seemed to come out of an angry reluctance. "I've never been assigned to this particular occupation before."

Deadalus had a glimmer of understanding.

"There are other roles that the women play then?"

"A few."

"And what was yours?"

She walked back around him into the room, not answering.

"Look," Deadalus said, turning to watch her. "Why don't you tell me what exactly's bothering you? Maybe we can work out something."

She gave a short laugh and went over to the underwater window and looked out. After a moment of silence she spoke, still without looking at him.

"I am, or rather, was, Deadalus's oracle."

Deadalus felt a strange tingling sensation pass through him at her words. She seemed to have given a strange emphasis to the name Deadalus.

"You're what?"

"I tell his fortune." She glanced at him then looked away. "About a year ago he came to me in the middle of the night. He was quite distraught and said he'd been having horrible, vivid dreams. He wanted, he insisted that I tell him how he was to die. I tried to talk him out of it, tried to calm him down, but he was too upset. So I made the preparations. I read the signs and it said: 'Retrieved from the depth of space, Deadalus by Deadalus shall be slain.

He understood it to mean that after some accident in space he'd kill himself. And since then he's not gone off this planet in hopes of frustrating the prediction."

"It's possible to do that then? To counteract your prediction?"

She shrugged slightly.

"It sometimes seems so. But I think that it's usually a case of the prediction being misunderstood."

Deadalus realized that every muscle in his body had tensed and that he was taking short, quick breaths as if he'd just run a mile. He tried to get himself to calm down.

"This was a year ago?"

"Yes. Then yesterday he asked me to see what I could find out about you. The way you were found made him think that maybe you were significant. He's a great believer in signs. So I cast your fortune. After reading it I tried to tell him that you were not significant to him, that your future and his do not interact. He knew I was lying. He kept after me but I told him the same thing. So he decided to put me in here with you."

There were a hundred questions that Deadalus wanted to ask Clea, but first he wanted to think over and digest what she had already told him. Everything seemed to be becoming increasingly complicated. As if caught in some invisible multistranded web, every move he made seemed to entangle him more and more.

He wandered around the room for a few minutes and then came to a stop in the doorway that led into the adjoining room. He looked at the large, sunken tub.

"Hey, how do you fill this thing?" he asked, stepping down into it to look it over.

"You open the stops on either end. Left is hot, right cold," she answered, coming into the doorway behind him. "But you have to get undressed first or you'll get all wet. Here, I'll show you."

She unzipped her jumpsuit and stepped out of it. Deadalus looked at her and was about to say something about too many complications, but then he took a second look and changed his mind.

chapter twelve

It was a memorable bath. And after they were through, they moved back out onto the bed which proved to be much more comfortable then it looked.

Deadalus sat up. He had dozed off. One of the gas lights had gone out and the other two were flickering. He got up and went over to the nearest one. It went out completely before he figured out that it worked on a simple pressure valve and merely had to be pumped up. He pumped up the third but couldn't find anything to light the first two with, and so gave up and went back to the bed.

He looked down at Clea where she lay sprawled on the covers. She had a very intriguing body. Though not proportioned as the fashion world would prefer, her body had character. Her hips were thin and bony, her arms, legs, and stomach hard with muscle. Her complete ease with her nakedness had surprised him and Deadalus was learning that Clea was completely unpredictable.

She opened her eyes and caught him staring

at her. Deadalus smiled. She just looked back at him without smiling.

"Can we talk?" he asked.

"I don't like talking."

"Yes. So I've noticed. But there are some things which are rather important that I'd like to discuss."

She turned over on her stomach and he sat down on the bed next to her.

"How do you do your fortune telling?"

"Two ways. I do it by gazing at anything shiny or even a bowl of water. That's one way. But for important things I use the fish."

"The fish? You mean in that aquarium out there? How do you go about that?"

"Catch one, slaughter it, and read the signs on its insides."

"You said that you lied to Deadalus about what you saw in my fortune. Why?"

"I wasn't sure if I wanted him to know what I had seen."

"What had you seen?"

"Not a lot. It's difficult to tell the fortune of someone who is not present and whom I've never met and know practically nothing about."

"But you did see something. What was it? What was it that you didn't want him to know?"

She sat up quickly and pulled a blanket around her, glaring at him while she did so.

"That wasn't what I said. If you're going to ask questions you ought to pay more attention to the answers. I said I wasn't sure if I wanted him to know what I had learned. I'm still not sure. I had to think about it and so I lied to him."

"What was it that you saw?" he prodded.

"If I wouldn't tell him, who has all the power, why should I tell you, who are power-less?"

"Why would you have told me this much if you weren't planning to tell me?" he reasoned.

She suddenly smiled. "Good. You are think-ing. I was afraid that you were as dull-witted as you let on. What I saw was simply that you are also Deadalus. That's all I saw and don't ask me what it means because I haven't been able to figure it out. All I know is that in the fish both you and he were given the same sign. Does it mean anything to you?"

Her change of mood had once again caught Deadalus off balance. Her question had been well calculated and he knew it. He could think of a hundred good reasons not to answer it. For all he knew she had been put here with the sole purpose of getting information out of him. His intuitions denied this, and whenever in doubt he always trusted his hunches. Besides, if the pirate boss did know all that she had just told him then there really wasn't too much left to hide.

"My name is Deadalus."

She leaned back against the wall at the head of the bed and thought.

"I think it must mean more than that. I think the two of you must have more in common than a name."

"Why didn't you tell Deadalus?"

She looked up at the ceiling for a while without answering. When she once again spoke her voice had a faraway sound.

131

"When I tell fortunes what I see is really just a future possibility. There are always more than one possibilities, but the number is always limited. If there is an important decision on hand in the life of the person I'm forcasting for, the possibilities may be no more than two. At other times they may go up to a dozen. But never much more than that. The possible outcomes are always a direct result of some choice being made. Of course there are a million choices that a person makes every day, but because every choice you're faced with today is the result of all the choices you made in the past, most of the choices will lead to the same, far-off conclusion. When there are a number of possible conclusions the one which has the greatest number of choices leading to it is the one that appears the strongest to me. But whatever I see in the future is not a foregone conclusion. And whenever I'm looking into the future I'm never sure that I see all the possibilities. One of the future possibilities I've seen is Deadalus sitting at the head of an empirical tyranny."

She paused and looked directly at him.

"But that's not why I wouldn't tell him about you. The reason is because, in that vision, I've seen myself sitting right by his side as his queen and consort."

A violent shudder shook her shoulders. Deadalus reached over to steady her but she got up and walked over to the underwater window and stared out.

"And you think that I might be able to help you turn away that possibility."

"That's what I thought. But now I'm not at all certain. See, when I had forecast his death for him and it had said that Deadalus shall be by Deadalus slain, it made sense at the time to think that it meant suicide. But when you turned up I realized that he could be mistaken in interpreting it like that. My first thought was that it meant that you were come here to kill him."

"And you don't think that now?"

"Don't you see? Both interpretations can be wrong. Your sign is exactly the same as his. When it says that Deadalus is to kill Deadalus, how can I tell which one of you it means?"

Deadalus thought about it and then smiled.

"Well, I guess that just means you can't forecast the outcome. There is still a lot you can do to influence the way things are going to turn out."

"Don't get too presumptious. I'm not necessarily for you. I'm just against him."

"Why are you so opposed to him?"

"He's pure evil. And he's powerful. Everyone has some evil in them, but he's all evil and he can bring it out in you. I can feel myself becoming more and more evil the longer I'm around him. And that vision I had where he was the empirical ruler and I was his consort, I saw that I had become just as evil as him."

She turned around to look at Deadalus where he was still sitting on the bed.

"And the worst thing is that I already feel tempted. Sometimes when I'm with him I think that I want to become his queen and take all that power. I can already feel the temptation. He's got to be killed."

She spoke in an intense whisper as if trying desperately to convince herself.

"Why do you think he put you in here with me? It sounds like he should suspect it could work against him."

"He did it just to show how powerful he is. That's his one great weakness. He's always doing things just to prove his strength. He put me in here just to show that he doesn't fear either of us. He's always doing these uselessly difficult things. And he always succeeds."

"So far."

Her mouth turned down in disgust.

"Oh great, another boaster! That's all I need!"

Deadalus was about to ask her something but looking at her he suddenly forgot what it was.

"Why don't you come back to bed for a while," he suggested.

She looked at him, surprised, and then started laughing.

"Always trying to prove something, aren't you?"

"Just come here, lady and I'll show you it's no idle boast."

She did. And he did.

All the next day Deadalus stayed in the room expecting the pirate boss to send for him. The wait made him think. And thinking made him worry.

The situation was bad and he cursed himself for having been too impulsive. There were a lot of easier ways he could have gotten to the bottom of this. In fact he could have just left the whole thing alone and eventually the Empirical government would have caught up with the pirates. The man was obviously over-reaching himself, and the more he over-reached the quicker he would be caught.

But there was no denying that he had become increasingly intrigued with his evil counter-part, and now that he was here he might as well see the thing through. Still there was no reason for him to take more risks than necessary.

When evening came and there had still been no word, Deadalus could wait no longer. He was going to try and get word to the *Orpheus*. Once he knew that they had his location and were on their way he'd feel much better.

Clea watched him as he checked the gun which they had given him on the ship and taped his knife to his arm.

"I have to send a message. Do you know where I might find an unguarded terminal?"

"All the terminals are on the second floor in the east section. I've no idea if they're guarded. I've never been anywhere near them."

He finished getting ready and went to the door.

"Any last bit of advice?" he asked.

She looked at him and then turned her back.

"I know nothing about warfare."

"OK. I'll see you later then, Clea."

She didn't answer him as he left.

Deadalus tried to calm his jumpy nerves as he walked down the narrow hallway. No one had told him to stay in his room and as far as he knew he was free to wander around. There was no reason why he should attract any attention at all unless he wandered into some section that was generally off limits.

He tried to retrace the route he'd been brought by, but after a few minutes he realized that he must have taken a wrong turn and was irrevocably lost. The building seemed to consist of nothing but long, thin hallways that twisted around themselves like an old city's streets. Here and there were stairways, as thin and crooked as the halls.

Most of the rooms he passed had their doors closed, but here and there one of them would be open. Inside Deadalus saw living quarters similar to his own, and occasionally a pirate or two. Deadalus nodded but, not knowing anyone, passed on without asking for directions.

He tried to keep in a generally eastern direction but he was soon so turned around that he concentrated on merely getting down to the second floor.

Finally he came to a large room where there were a great many men playing cards or drinking or watching various things on large view screens. Deadalus saw someone he knew from the ship and went over and asked for directions. The man laughed and gave him easy to follow instructions. Deadalus got to the second floor with no more trouble and headed toward the east section.

The rooms here were of a different nature. They were larger without doors, and filled with various machines. There were a number of people about and no one seemed to pay any particular attention to Deadalus, so he stepped into one of the rooms and looked at the equipment.

The machines were very odd-looking and none of them seemed to be working. A few of them were opened up as if for repairs and the others stood about, dusty and unused. Deadalus was at first puzzled until he realized that the machines were ancient. They were as old as the building itself, mere remnants of a civilization that had killed itself off with its own technology. A technology which perhaps held secrets that the empirical empire hadn't yet rediscovered.

Deadalus moved on looking for a terminal in a secluded area. The first two he came across were in too open of a location. He wasn't sure that he'd be questioned if he used one, but he didn't want to take that risk unless he had to, so he worked his way from room to room, deeper into the maze.

Finally he located a terminal in and out of the way alcove in one of the rooms. He put in his message to the *Orpheus,* telling them the location of the planet, and as much as he knew about the pirate's defenses. He programmed the message to be sent and left the room, feeling greatly relieved.

He figured it would take about a day after they received the message for the starship to reach him. He decided to go back to the game room and see what kind of information he could pick up. On his way he passed by a small doorway and heard some voices animatedly discussing something. He paused to listen. Unable to make out what was being said he was just about to move on when he heard someone behind him.

He looked over his shoulder and found five pairs of not so friendly eyes glaring at him. Beneath which were five even less friendly gun muzzles.

chapter thirteen

"Don't move," one of them commanded.

Deadalus had no intention of moving. The five guns were held by five pirates all of whom were wearing green silk armbands.

One of the men came forward and, making certain not to stand between Deadalus and the guns trained on him, removed Deadalus's gun from its belt holster.

"Don't get excited, boys. I guess I got a little bit lost. If I've wandered somewhere I'm not supposed to be, I do apologize. But let's not get carried away."

The men made no reply but simply gestured that he was to proceed them into the room that the voices had been coming from.

There were three men in the room, two of whom Deadalus already knew. One was the red-headed captain of the ship that had picked him up. The other was the captain of the second ship. The third man had his back to the room and was staring out an underwater window similar to the one in Deadalus's room.

The red-headed captain stared at Deadalus

with surprise and then his look changed to rage. Deadalus noted this and figured it was a bad sign, but all of his attention was on the third man he knew must be the pirate boss.

The man was deceptively tall and thin. He had that type of physique which was like a steel spring. Though not bulging with muscles, it was as hard as steel and as quick as a whip. Perhaps the most surprising feature that Deadalus could discern from the back was that the pirate boss was completely bald.

"We caught this guy sneaking around. It looked like he was listening in."

The pirate boss turned around and glanced at Deadalus distractedly. He had dark, deepset eyes, a sharp nose, thin lips, and a black goatee.

"Who is he? Did you ask him what he was doing?"

"He said he was lost."

"This is the man we were just talking about," the red-headed captain interrupted. "He's the guy we picked up out in space."

"Indeed!" The bald-headed pirate leader suddenly became very interested. He clasped his hands behind his back and walked over to look closely in Deadalus's face.

"Well, this saves me the trouble of having to send for you. It seems we've got a little problem and you're just the man to help us. What do you say? Want to help us?"

Deadalus looked at him curiously and glanced back over at the five men who all still had their guns on him.

"I don't want to cause a heart attack. Everyone around here seems a might jumpy. But like I said, I got turned around, not an impossible thing to do in this place. I heard some voices and I thought I might ask my way."

The goateed pirate bent forward so that his face was a few inches from Deadalus's.

"Just a coincidence, huh? Like you being right in my ship's path to be picked up? Just a coincidence. Like you picking up that girl and thinking we should ransom her. Just a coincidence, right?"

"Hey, I'm in the middle of space in a lifeboat, you can't mean I intended . . ."

Deadalus froze as the tall man whipped out a gun from behind his back and pressed it against Deadalus's right temple.

The pirate leaned even closer and bared his teeth in an evil grin.

"And you think we should ransom her, is that right?"

Deadalus chose his words carefully. There was evidently something about the girl which had the pirates upset and Deadalus didn't know what.

"It was just an idea. I really don't care what you do with her."

"It's fine with you if we just smash her head in?"

"If that's what you do with girls around here."

"Who is she?"

"She said her name was Syndy Ellington. Commander Ellington's daughter."

"She did, did she? And you believe her?"

"I couldn't see any reason for her to lie. It must be a pretty easy thing to check out."

"Of course. And what would you say if I told

141

you that she's the third female in a month who has claimed to be the daughter of a high official. The third. And all three wanted us to ransom them. What do you say to that?"

Deadalus felt a cold chill run down his back. He could feel the gun pressing hard against his temple and he could see from the other's eyes that there would be no hesitation in shooting him.

"If what you say is true, I'd say it's a plot."

"Good." The pirate nodded. "And just who is it that is behind this plot?"

"The only people that could carry off something like that would be the Empirical secret police."

"Very good. I'm glad we've had this little chat. Now, last question and then you can be on your way. With all of your amazing coincidences, all the things you've done since my men first picked you up, what is there to make me believe you're not a member of the secret police?"

Deadalus knew that he could probably get the gun away from the pirate. He still had his knife, he might even be able to kill him. But with five guns aimed and ready to fire he'd only live about ten seconds. And Deadalus preferred to live a little longer then that. Besides, he had an answer the bald-headed man would probably believe.

The truth.

"I can't be involved in the plot by the secret police because I'm the man they were plotting against."

The pirate blinked.

"How's that?"

"My name is Deadalus and it's only because they thought that you were me that they would concoct such a plot."

The pirate straightened up but kept the gun level, a look of almost horror replacing his grin.

"What did you say your name was?"

"The same as yours. Deadalus. I was a member of the secret police once. We had a falling out and I've been having a running battle with them ever since."

"Hey, I've heard of you!" It was the red-headed captain who now spoke. "I thought you were just a myth though."

Deadalus waited, watching his evil namesake. The pirate seemed thrown off balance by this information. But it was only a brief moment. Then he grinned again.

"Very, very good. But you're lying. Clea told you to say that, didn't she? She's behind all of this."

"Of course not. Why would I put myself in her hands? That's not even logical. If I'm not who I say I am, then who am I?"

The pirate leader laughed.

"All right, let's assume you are this Deadalus character. I don't believe it, but it will be easy to verify. But tell me, if you are this guy who's rumored to fly about helping out the poor and helpless and fighting their overwhelming oppressor, if you are this Deadalus, what are you doing here?"

"I just wanted to see who was ruining my good name."

The pirate's right hand whipped out violently and struck Deadalus across the face. Deadalus was able to turn with the backhanded blow, depriving it of most of its force so that it merely stung him rather than the teeth-jarring blow it had been intended to be.

"You're going to have to do better than that," the tall pirate said softly.

Deadalus looked at him steadily, then shrugged.

"There really isn't much more to it than that. I was almost lynched by a bunch of people who blamed me for the things you were doing. I thought that it might be something instigated by the secret police. I thought that if I was going to be killed I wanted it to be for something I had done, not for something you had done. I wanted to resolve the situation so I came here to see what I could do about it."

"So you came here all by yourself just to clear your name. That's almost dumb enough to be true. Almost." The pirate paused, looking Deadalus over thoughtfully. "There are methods of extracting information, methods which can break any man, even you. But I think I can make better use of you, I don't want to waste you unless I have to. Besides, there's an easier way of getting the information. Whoever you are and whatever it is your really after, I'm sure that Clea is behind it. I think it'll be much easier to get the information out of her than out of you."

The pirate turned to the five men behind Deadalus and was about to give an order when a sharp paging tone came from the computer console over in the corner. The bald-headed pirate tried to talk over it, but the tone continued and so, impatiently, he strode over to the computer to take care of it.

Deadalus took a deep breath to steady himself and carefully looked around. The two pirate captains were still where they were when Deadalus had been brought in. The one looked somewhat bored while the red-headed one from the ship that Deadalus had been on looked extremely uncomfortable. He would not look at Deadalus but stared off at the far wall. Of the five men in green armbands only three remained, but they still had their guns in hand, diligently waiting for orders. Deadalus concluded that they must be some sort of select honor guard or private policing force within the main body of the pirates. The existence of a private guard underlined the fact that this was no mere pirate that he was dealing with. This man who shared Deadalus's name seemed to have the intention of becoming some kind of king. The intention and, apparently, the capabilities.

The pirate leader returned form the computer console, his face a cloud of unreadable emotions.

"You three get back to your stations," he said to the remaining guards and then turned to the two captains. "More information has come up that changes the color of this whole thing. I'll get back to you later on it. For now just keep the men occupied, maybe get more hunting parties organized or something."

The two captains rose and the one left. But the red-headed captain lingered.

The pirate boss looked at him quizzically.

"Is there something the matter, Captain?"

"I'm not sure," the captain hesitated. "This may have nothing to do with anything but while we were on our way back home here I, uh, sort of blundered into a trap set up by the army. We would have been dead for sure except this man here got us out of it," he said, nodding in Deadalus's direction.

The captain then gave a brief recounting of the incident and the role that Deadalus played in it.

"I didn't report it before," the captain concluded, "because I didn't think it was that important and, quite frankly, I felt embarrassed about how I had handled it. So maybe he's who he says he is, I don't know. I just thought it might have some bearing."

The captain nodded to the bald-headed pirate, glanced sympathetically at Deadalus, and left. The black-bearded pirate turned to Deadalus.

"Sit down, Captain Deadalus, and let's talk."

Deadalus tensed at the other's use of his name and rank, but did as he was bidden. The pirate however remained standing, staring down at him.

"I must admit you did have me puzzled. You still do, in a way. What I couldn't understand is how you could come here like this, being who you are, and be so bold and careless. Nor could I understand how, if you were Deadalus, you could possibly afford to tell me so. But now I understand. Any man with a secret police starship waiting to come and rescue him would bound to feel a bit invulnerable."

146

Deadalus felt his stomach muscles knot. The pirate grinned evilly.

"The only problem is that no broadcasts are made from this planet without first being cleared through me. A pretty good precaution, wouldn't you say? Otherwise your starship *Orpheus* might have already been on its way here. That rather changes the complexion of things, wouldn't you agree?"

chapter fourteen

Deadalus cursed himself. He couldn't believe
that he had become so careless. Not so much
for not having considered that his broadcast
would be intercepted and stopped, but more for
having made his plans rely so heavily on the
starship being able to rescue him. If he was
going to work alone he should not have made
his plans dependent on anyone other than
himself. He must be getting old.

And if he hoped to get any older he was
going to have to come up with an alternative plan.
And pretty quick.

"You seem to have suddenly run dry on your
snappy replies," the pirate said, still grinning.
"Maybe now you'll be a little more cooperative."

"What are you talking about?"

"I'm in the process of starting up a new society,
a society outside of and independent of the present Empirical government. I'm starting it right
here on this planet. It's an enormous task and
I can use all the good help I can get. I would
like you to join forces with me."

"What's the catch?"

"No catch. Both of my captains were once captains of ships that were opposing me. The proposition is really quite simple. Either you join up with me or you'll be killed."

Deadalus looked at him skeptically.

"And how do you insure that I won't turn on you at the first opportunity?"

"I don't give you the opportunity. I take precautions of course, and after a while I think you'll find that it's to your best benefit to be on my side. If I gave any of the men, even my two captains, the choice now of staying with me or going out on their own, all of them would choose to stay. None of them can do so well by themselves as I can do for them."

While the pirate was talking Deadalus was casually shifting his feet so that they were pressed firmly against the floor beneath him. He was at a great disadvantage. He had only a knife and he was sitting down while the other man was standing and holding a gun. But Deadalus didn't doubt that he'd never get as good of an opportunity.

"That's a very interesting proposition," he said to keep the other talking. "What kind of position are you offering me?"

"The way I see it you would be second in command in charge of the defenses. You'd still be in command of the starship, though my men would crew it."

"In charge of defenses?" Deadalus leaned forward, shifting his weight to his feet and crossing his arms, working his hand closer to his knife. "You really are trying to build a second empire?"

150

"Trying? No, not just merely trying. It's already well on its way."

The tall pirate turned and walked over to the underwater window and looked out. Deadalus took the opportunity to work his knife loose and let it slide down his sleeve to his palm.

"I've got so much power now that no one is going to be able to stop me." He turned around so that he was facing Deadalus again. "You see, the original society on this planet developed a technology that was greater than they could control and it wiped them out. They're gone, but their technology remains. It remains here on this planet, hidden in the bits and pieces that they left. And I've spent the last year ferreting out the secrets of that advanced technology. It seemed like an impossible task at first, like a monkey trying to figure out a computer. But I kept at it. I told myself that they were men just like me and that anything they could know, I too could learn. And piece by piece I've been reconstructing it. Every new thing I uncovered in turn began to aid me. The method for getting those old cruisers to fly faster, a method for jamming all radio broadcasts from an entire planet, and more. I've just barely scratched the surface of all that this place has to offer and already I'm too powerful for the Empirical government to stop."

"It doesn't sound as if you need me, then."

"Need you?" The pirate laughed scornfully. "No, of course I don't need you. I said I could use you. The more good men I have the easier it is. But I don't *need* you. I don't need anyone." The bearded pirate shook himself and stood up straight. "But that doesn't matter right now. Your choice is simple, you can either join up with me or be killed. Don't decide right now; I'll give you some time to think about it. And I've got a special place designed just for thinking about these things."

As the pirate grinned at him, Deadalus leaned slightly to the left to get his knife hand open. It was the slightest of motions, but even before he could complete it the other's gun was up and aimed at his head.

"Move one finger more and you won't get the luxury of making a choice," the pirate said from between his teeth.

Deadalus didn't move as the pirate boss called in the guards, two of whom pinned his arms back while the third relieved him of his knife.

The pirate boss took the knife and with his bare hands snapped the blade off at the hilt. Then he walked over to Deadalus and grabbed him by the throat with one hand and squeezed until Deadalus's face turned blue. Leaning close, he grinned.

"Next time you decide to try and take me on, do me the honor of not underestimating me."

Deadalus opened his eyes, hoping that he was dead. He blinked. Opening his eyes had made no change in the total blackness. Then the smell hit him again.

He gagged and had to struggle to keep himself from retching. The blackness was filled with the overpowering stench of rotting flesh.

When they had opened the door to put him

in and he had caught the first whiff of that smell Deadalus had fought back as best he could. But his hands had already been bound behind him and they were too many of them. Still, they hadn't been able to get him inside until after they had beaten him unconscious.

He blocked the smell out of his mind as best he could and concentrated on doing what he could to free his hands. He got awkwardly to his feet and shuffled along until he bumped into the wall and then he sat down again. He felt around until he had found a fairly rough spot on the stone wall behind him and began to rub the binding on his wrists against it. The binding was made of some sort of tough cord and Deadalus had no idea how long it would take to wear through it. Nor did he have any idea if it would do him the least bit of good even if he could get his hands free. But he wanted to be doing something and he couldn't think of anything else to do.

He thought back over the recent events. He wasn't sure how much of what he'd been told was true. He wasn't about to take everything the pirate said at face value. One thing he was sure of though, things really had taken on a different complexion since his message to the *Orpheus* had been intercepted. Still, they probably wouldn't have connected him with the message if it hadn't have been for Syndy.

Had he been anywhere other than where he was, Deadalus probably would have found it funny that he and an agent for the secret police had been sharing a room together without either of them realizing it. But if what the pirate boss had said was true, the young lady must certainly have been planted by the secret police. It was just the smooth kind of operation that Hissler liked to use. And it would have worked too, except for the confusion of the two Deadalus's. It was a trap designed for him, but it was impotent against someone of the pirate Deadalus's nature. Things would have turned out a lot different if he had not gotten involved with her.

Deadalus tried to think of what options he had left. There was Clea, but he felt really uncertain about her. He wasn't sure how much, if any of what she told him was actually true. She could have easily been planted there by the pirate. Or she could be working on her own, trying to play the one of them against the other.

Deadalus scraped his knuckles against the wall and paused for a moment to rest. The smell of something dead and rotting was so strong he could taste it. He wasn't sure how big the room was, but he figured that it couldn't be to big and he was certain that there wasn't going to be any magical trapdoors to get him out.

He pulled at his bonds and was surprised to feel them give a little. He started up scraping again.

There was of course the option that the pirate boss himself had offered. He could join up with them. Deadalus would consider it, even if just for a way to play for time, except that he knew the first thing he'd have to do would be

to call the *Orpheus* and have all the crew surrender to the same fate as himself.

Deadalus thought of Rhea and her idealism
and of Whiskey and his sincerity. They would
never agree to go along with what the pirate
was doing. And then they too would just end
up being tortured to death. No, he couldn't
even pretend to go along with the pirate if it
meant getting the rest of his crew involved.

He pulled at his bonds again and this time
they stretched enough for him to be able to
work free. He rubbed the circulation back into
his wrists and wondered what to do next. He
imagined that the wait wouldn't be too long.
He had the feeling that the pirate wouldn't
rest until the situation with him was resolved.

He thought about Clea's prediction that one
Deadalus would kill the other and tried to
figure out where that would fit in. If what she
said was true, how much would it affect the
pirate? From all that Deadalus had seen and
heard about the pirate, he was willing to believe that Clea had been telling the truth.
Superstition was just the kind of quirk that
would fit in with the pirate's nature. So many
major figures of history, both great and in-
famous, had been superstitious. It had to do
with their illusions of grandeur and egocen-
tricity. They couldn't believe that their lives
were affected by anything so petty as chance
and luck. Everything that happened to them
had to be the work of some god.

If Clea had predicted that one of them would
kill the other, the pirate wouldn't chance leaving Deadalus alive for very long, it would seem

too risky. So that offer to have him join up had probably just been a ploy, a method of trying to get the *Orpheus*. Once the pirate possessed that, he'd probably kill Deadalus. Or then again, maybe not.

Deadalus rubbed the side of his head. Everything was so tangled up, there was no way that he was going to be able to just think his way through it. He knew too little, and too much of what he did know could very likely be false.

The smell was getting to him. Even though he was breathing shallowly through his mouth and applying all his training to try and block it from his mind, it was just too overpowering. Maybe if he could turn on a light and be able to see what and where the dead animal was, that might help.

He carefully stood up. Every room that he had been in had a lantern on the wall on the right side of the door. Since there were no windows it made sense to have a light in ready reach whenever you entered a room. That of course did not guarantee that this room would have one or that if it did it would still be in working condition. But there was one way to find out.

He started shuffling along next to the wall, his hand feeling along its worn surface. He imagined with every step that he was going to walk into a pile of rotting bones and flesh. It seemed as if the smell was growing stronger with each step but he knew that was just his imagination. The smell was already so strong, even if it did get stronger his nose wouldn't be able to distinguish the difference.

He came to a corner and turned and started off in the new direction. Finally he came to a crease in the wall that felt like the door. He felt around where the lights usually were and sure enough there was one. It felt all right and so he pumped it up as he had done with the ones in his room. Now to light it.

He couldn't remember having seen anyone use any sort of lighter, so there must be some way on the lantern itself to get it to light. As it used some sort of liquid or gas fuel a simple sparking mechanism would be logical. He felt around on the lantern and in a moment found exactly what he was looking for. He pushed the sparking device a couple times and the lantern flickered and then came to life. Deadalus turned it up as bright as it would go and then turned around.

He almost wished he hadn't.

The room, as he had suspected, was quite small, about ten feet long by eight feet wide. It was made of the same block stone as the rest of the building and was completely featureless except for another lantern on the opposing wall. The ceiling of the room was quite high, and hanging from it on large hooks, were three bodies in various stages of decomposing. In the corner was a dusty pile of bones which apparently had fallen from a fourth hook when all of its flesh had rotted away.

The three bodies were hanging so that their feet dangled only a few inches above Deadalus's head. The hooks that held them were three pronged, two of the prongs going through from the back and hooking under the collar bone and the third, smaller hook driven into the back of the skull to hold it in an upright position. They were all three unclothed and it was easy to see that they had been there a various amount of time.

The oldest body, not counting the pile of bones on the floor, looked to be a number of years old. It was dried and shrunken, its hair out in patches and its eyes gone.

The newest body could not have been over a day old. It was a female, though no one that Deadalus recognized. From what he could see she had been dead before being placed on the hooks as there was no blood from the wounds where the hooks poked through. Her eyes and mouth were open in a look of unspeakable horror.

It was the third body which was causing the sickening smell. Dead for a number of months, the flesh was open and oozing. The abdomen had burst and was covered with a thick green mold. Even in the light from the one lantern Deadalus could discern the small white worms which covered the sores and no doubt filled the body.

Deadalus sat down slowly and stared down at the floor between his feet. He had seen a great number of dead and mangled bodies in his time, but that did not make this sight any prettier nor make the thought of being confined in this room any more delightful.

What bothered him most was that there seemed to be no sane reason for the spectacle.

The people had apparently been already dead before they'd been hung on the hooks. The only possible use for it could be as a sort of psychological torture, a method of punishment for people who got out of line. Deadalus could imagine that after spending a night in here with these bodies people would have a tendency to be a lot more cooperative.

Deadalus thought about the twisted workings of the mind that could conceive of such a method of discipline. He was beginning to understand what Clea had meant when she had said that the pirate boss was pure evil. And he understood that surprising tone of fear in the big red-headed captain when he'd told Deadalus not to fool around with the pirate.

This room was no doubt just the first step. The sick mind that had thought of this would most likely have many other forms of torture to revel in. Tortures which, even with Deadalus's years of experience with the secret police, he couldn't conceive of.

Deadalus lay down facing the wall and closed his eyes. He forced his body to relax, to rejuvenate and restore his energy. He was going to need every ounce of strength he had. He was going to have to make sure that his mind was quick and clear. He wanted to make certain that the next time he came up against the pirate Deadalus he wouldn't be the one to underestimate his opponent.

He had slept off and on for maybe eight hours when he was brought instantly alert by the sound of the door grating open.

chapter fifteen

The man standing in the door held a gun in one hand and a cloth over his nose and mouth with the other. He motioned with the gun for Deadalus to come out.

Deadalus smiled.

"Oh, do come in. I was just about to serve some tea."

The man turned slightly green and fired his laser, searing the wall next to Deadalus's head. Two other guards appeared behind the first and Deadalus forgot his ideas of trying to fight his way out.

He allowed himself to be ushered out of the room and down a long dark hallway. He noticed that the three guards shied away from him and realized that he must smell pretty bad. His own sense of smell had become too adjusted to tell.

The three guards, all of whom had their guns in hand, said nothing and if they were surprised that his hands were unbound they didn't show it. They were extremely cautious, at all times making sure to stay out of his

161

reach and in position to have a clean shot at him should he make any false move.

Deadalus walked slowly despite the guards' attempts to hurry him up. He made note of and memorized everything he could see, every door and passageway they passed.

The hallway they were in came to an end in another passageway. Deadalus stopped and looked to the right and left. The right-hand side went down a stairway at the bottom of which Deadalus saw a pale light. The guards barked at him to go to the left, but Deadalus took two steps to the right just to get a better look.

Three lasers simultaneously burnt the floor in front of him and he turned back around with a smile and went in the direction they indicated. But he'd gotten a good enough look to be certain that the light at the bottom of the stairs had not been cast by any lantern. It had been sunlight.

They went down three more hallways and up two different stairways but Deadalus was certain he could retrace his steps if need be. Finally he was ushered into a room which looked like some sort of laboratory. The pirate Deadalus was standing on the far side in front of a large window that appeared to look into another small room. He turned around as Deadalus was brought in.

The three guards took up positions around the room. They were not going to give Deadalus any chance whatsoever to try and escape.

The pirate wrinkled his nose as he caught a whiff of Deadalus.

"I hope you've come to realize that you've everything to gain by joining up with me, and everything to lose if you don't."

The pirate's voice and manner was of one who is certain of his power and sure of the outcome. Deadalus felt a slow, obstinate fire in his stomach.

"Not exactly."

"What do you mean?" the pirate frowned.

"Obviously if it was just myself I would take up your offer, if only to try and later escape. But I've the feeling that your offer isn't quite as simple as that."

"Of course. I want the starship and your crew."

"That's the problem. I can't bring my crew into your grasp. And they need the starship in order to survive. So I guess that's that." Deadalus smiled.

The pirate glared, clasped his hands behind his back and started pacing.

"Why are you so worried about your crew? They're just as well off serving me as serving you. One boss is the same as another to a pirate. All they worry about is getting fed."

"My crew members aren't pirates. Outlaws maybe, but not pirates."

The tall, bearded Deadalus scoffed.

"Petty semantics. Call yourself what you will, we're both fighting the same enemy, aren't we? We both seek to tear down the Empirical government, don't we? And we both do it by the same means. We take what we need where we can get it. You may fool your men with all sorts of noble prattle, but don't try to give that stuff to me." His voice was loud and angry.

"We may have a mutual enemy, but we don't have the same cause." Deadalus's voice was as angry as the pirate's. "I and my men are fighting to free ourselves of a tyranny. You're merely trying to supplant one tyrant with another."

The pirate stopped pacing about ten feet in front of Deadalus. His face and bald head were red with anger.

"Oh? And what is it that you propose to replace the Empirical government with? Or aren't you already putting yourself above by your actions! Who nominated you for the job of savior?"

"I wasn't nominated for anything!" Deadalus shouted back. "We were forced to fight or die."

"Any cheap bandit can say the same."

"You're simply after your own self gain. I'm fighting for the good of the whole."

"Who says? Who told you that? Did the people of the galaxy all get together and send you a note saying that they needed you to fight for them? Or didn't you just take it upon yourself to set yourself above the law, to consider yourself exempt from the accepted government! Don't give me that crap about the good of the whole. We're talking about the difference between a publicly given role and a self-chosen one. And in that there is no difference between you and I. We have both assumed the right to put ourselves above the common law."

"When the law is corrupt . . ."

"But who's deciding the law's corrupt? You're deciding that! And it's by believing that you

can see better what is for the good of the masses
than they themselves can see that you're putting yourself above them. Look," the pirate
tried to calm himself, "there's two sets of rules.
There are the rules that the masses live by,
and there are the rules which the few self-
chosen leaders live by. That's the way it's always been. You chose to put yourself above
the common law. Now, regardless of what it is
you've decided to fight for, it was your decision,
it was not something you were elected to do.
When you give me that trash about the public
good, what you mean is what *you* have decided
is for the public good. It's your self-chosen goal
that you're fighting for. And if my chosen goal
is different than your's, that doesn't make you
any more in the right. You're fighting for yourself the same as I. The only difference is that
you're pretending that your goal is in the
public's best interest while I refuse to fool myself with such simple-minded sophistries."

"There's a difference between good and evil."

The pirate's face became stone hard. For a
moment he didn't speak, and when he did his
voice was quiet, sharp, and brittle.

"Oh, so you're going to be the one to decide
the difference between good and evil, are you?
You think you're the one to tell me the difference, that you can always pick the good
from the evil. We'll see about that. Come over
here."

The pirate turned and went back over to the
window and after a moment Deadalus followed.
The room that the window looked into was
small and had a number of instruments and

mechanisms on the walls. On the ledge in front of the pirate were a number of knobs and switches.

The pirate pushed one of the switches and a small door on the far wall sprung open. Deadalus could see something moving just beyond and in a moment it came out into the observation room.

It was a medium sized monkey of sorts and Deadalus surmised that it was the same animal that the hunting party killed for pelts. It moved cautiously, looking around with large, intelligent eyes. When it had moved a few steps out into the room, the pirate pushed another button and the door sprung shut again behind it.

"Now watch up on the ceiling."

Deadalus looked and saw a small glass tube descend into the room above the monkey's head. Looking closely he could see a small amount of liquid in it. He looked over at the pirate.

The pirate was grinning, but it was not a look of glee. He was still tense with anger and his eyes glittered with the look of a man who could hang bodies on hooks just for the fun of it.

"Watch closely now. I'm going to use just one small drop."

A drop of liquid appeared on the end of the tube, hung there for a second, and then dropped. It evaporated before it hit the floor. Deadalus could feel the blood pounding in his temples as he waited to see what would happen.

Thirty seconds after the liquid had entered the air of the closed room, the creature started running in circles, trying desperately to find some way out. It banged off the walls and floor, emitting a high squeal that was audible even through the thick glass of the observation window. Then it fell down in the middle of the floor, swatting at itself as if trying to drive off a swarm of insects. Then along the creature's legs and arms, Deadalus could see large red wounds appear. The fur fell out in clumps and the wounds expanded as if the skin was being melted off. Shocked and disgusted Deadalus looked over at the pirate who was watching the scene intensely.

"You think you know the difference between good and evil, do you?" The pirate spoke through clenched teeth without looking at him. "Well, here's a little test for you. You said you didn't feel right about delivering your crew over to me, that I'd be forcing them to serve some purpose that they didn't believe in. But that message you tried to send them is still in the computer and I've decided to have it broadcast."

Deadalus stiffened, catching his breath.

"And when your starship gets here I'm going to send out a module under a white flag. And on that module will be a container of this."

In the other room the monkey's skin had been completely disolved, exposing a bloody mass of muscles. And the monkey was still very much alive and thrashing about on the floor in obvious agony.

"The muscles and cartilage will begin to go next," the pirate said dryly. "The creature will remain alive for another seven minutes after that, but by then the brain will have been sufficiently dissolved that the creature will be unaware of its existence. So here is your choice." He turned and glared at Deadalus. "You can agree to serve me, turning over your crew and starship, or you will remain alive only long enough to hear their screams as they are literally skinned alive. Take a close look at that creature in there and let me hear you exercise your knowledge of good and evil."

chapter sixteen

Before Deadalus could even think to move he felt a gun in his back, silently dissuading him from attempting to attack the madman standing next to him. From the corner of his eye he could see that the other two guards had also begun to close in, guns held at ready.

Deadalus smiled grimly. Evidently the look on his face had been enough to clue them in to his reaction.

"What's your decision?" the pirate demanded. "Tell me what is good and what is evil. Make the choice. You think you can decide for other men, let's hear you decide."

Deadalus smiled. "Is there any antidote for that?" he asked, nodding his head to indicate the room where the creature lay twitching on the floor.

"None."

"Oh, good."

Deadalus smiled again at the pirate's puzzled expression and then leaped, whirling, and smashed his booted foot into the plate-glass observation window.

The glass splintered and fell to the floor with the sound of gently tinkling bells. Deadalus came down on top of the guard behind him, smashing him to the ground. But then the pirate boss caught Deadalus with a kick to the head, stunning him and knocking him momentarily unconscious.

The next thing he knew he was being dragged from the room and the door was slammed shut. Breathing heavily the pirate looked down at him furiously.

"I'll think of something extra special for that little trick." He turned to the two guards who were holding the third one up. "Take this scum back where you got him. And make sure he stays alive. I want the personal pleasure of seeing him die."

Deadalus was taken back downstairs and, after the guards had added a number more bruises to his already sore body, locked him back into the room with the rotting bodies.

Deadalus lay on the floor where they dumped him, trying to catch his breath. He hadn't really expected that trick with the window to work, but he couldn't think of anything better at the moment. Gingerly he moved his arms and legs, making sure that nothing was broken. If their leader hadn't specifically told them to leave him alive, Deadalus was sure that the guards would have finished him off before throwing him in here. Maybe hanging him up on the one empty hook to join the others.

Deadalus looked up at the hook, thinking. Quickly he got to his feet and pumped up the gas light. Then he crossed over and lit the second lamp as well. He peered up at the hook, trying to see how it was attached. The hook was at the end of a three-foot chain and the chain was somehow bolted to the ceiling. The light wasn't good enough for Deadalus to see exactly how it was connected or how difficult it would be to disconnect it. He'd have to get a closer look.

Backing up against the wall Deadalus took a couple running steps and leaped, but came up short by a few inches. He tried again, this time using the other wall to kick off from and he was able to grab hold of the hook. He pulled himself up and, putting his knees on the bottom hooks, was able to reach the ceiling.

He was in luck. The chain would come right off its ceiling mount simply by being lifted straight up, then twisted to the right. A simple enough maneuver, but one which he wouldn't be able to do while hanging on the chain at the same time.

He looked at the three bodies hanging from the other hooks. The thought of standing on top of one of them didn't exactly appeal to him, but he had no time to be squeamish. All the same, he chose the oldest body as the least repulsive of the three.

He swung the hook he was on until he could reach over and grab hold of the other chain. He swung himself onto the other chain, holding himself up so that he wasn't touching the body at all. He worked quickly to get the free chain unhooked but before he could his feet slipped and kicked the head beneath him. The head broke off and crashed to the floor. He mumbled an apology but took advantage of the accident, as it now allowed him to use the small upper hook for a sort of precarious perch.

He got the hook off and hefted it, feeling its weight. It was going to make a perfect weapon. He thought for a moment, considering his different options.

He shifted his weight to get a more secure hold and then swung the hook, smashing first one lamp and then the other. When the small room was black he started swinging the hook against the stone door.

The noise as the heavy steel hook hit the door was enormous and after three blows Deadalus could hear voices coming. He pulled the hook back up and waited.

The heavy stone door scraped open and one of the guards looked in. Unable to see anything, the guard cautiously stepped forward in the small patch of light let in by the open door. Deadalus swung the hook down with all his strength, smashing into the guard's head and knocking him into the corner.

The other guard fired his gun just out of reflex, not even having had the chance to see what happened. He called the first guard's name and, when he got no reply, began raking his laser around the walls, two feet from the floor. Deadalus waited tensely, but the second guard didn't seem to want to follow his friend. Deadalus decided he should move around to the other side of the chain he was hanging on in order to get a better angle. As he was doing so his foot slipped and his full weight came down on the dried up body hanging beneath him.

The already headless body fell and the guard shot it three times. Satisfied that he had just shot Deadalus, the guard stepped into the small room. Deadalus swung the hook. The guard somehow sensed the hook coming in the dark and stepped to the side. The hook, instead of hitting him in the head as Deadalus had intended pierced two prongs through the man's chest.

Deadalus was on the ground even before the man had stopped screaming. Picking up the guard's fallen laser he shot the guard who was writhing on the point of the hook, putting him out of his misery and putting an end to his screaming as well.

Deadalus searched the guard for any more weapons and found a long, two-edged knife which he stuck in his belt. He looked up and down the hallway and, seeing no one, started running in the direction which he knew would lead him out of the building.

When he reached the outer door Deadalus paused. Between the building and the jungle there was a hundred yards of cleared, open ground, well lit by floodlights. He was going to be an easy target if any guards happened to be watching. The only thing to Deadalus's advantage was that they would be guarding against attack, not escape. He hesitated a moment longer preparing himself and then the sound of pounding feet in the hallway behind him sparked him into motion.

He was three-fourths of the way across the clearing before the first shots came from behind him. He threw himself on the ground, rolled, and fired a shot back at the doorway before getting up and making another broken-field run toward the jungle. He dove into the thick vegetation, laser rays curling and smoking the leaves around his head. He rolled again, the vines and shrubs clutching at him. He could see a number of wild shots spitting into the jungle and he could hear the pirates across the open compound behind him.

Deadalus crawled struggling forward five, ten yards. The dense undergrowth ripped at his hands and clung to his clothes. He savagely pulled himself free, heedless of the scratches that tore across his skin. After twenty difficult yards of going straight forward Deadalus decided that he could risk standing up. Now he turned and moved parallel to the compound. Five minutes later he stopped to catch his breath and listen.

The jungle was thick and black around him. The floodlights from the compound had been swallowed up by the blackness. And though he was a stone's throw from the search party they could not see him, nor he them. But he could hear them quite plainly.

The pirates were half-heartedly searching straight ahead from the spot where Deadalus had entered the jungle. From what he heard Deadalus was certain that they were not able to pick up his trail in the dark. It also sounded as if they didn't really care. After a few more minutes of their stomping and cursing Deadalus heard the search called off.

"We won't find anything in the dark," he heard an authoritative voice say. "No use in us risking our necks. He'll be dead before we could find him anyways. We'll send a search party to find his body tomorrow."

Deadalus listened as the voices drifted away until finally there was silence. The thick smell of the vegetation enclosed him. He counted to a hundred, waiting, but there was no further sound of voices. Then he turned and carefully started working his way farther into the jungle. After a couple of minutes the tundra began to change. The brush and bramble gave way to a lower growing carpet of vines between knobby-trunked trees. The trees went up about a hundred feet and then branched out in such a tangle of interlocking limbs as to completely block off the sky. There was a faint luminescent glow which Deadalus could not at first account for until he saw that high above in the tree limbs there was a vine whose leaves gave off a faint blue-green glow. After awhile the light was strong enough so that he could see his footing.

The pirate's comment about the danger of the jungle had put Deadalus on his guard. He watched and listened for any possible sign though he had no idea what he was supposed to be looking for. Had he not been tensed to pick up any odd noise or motion he might have missed it when it came.

He stopped, holding his breath, listening. Somewhere nearby there had been a soft moan. It came again. Deadalus turned, gun ready, trying to see through the half-light. The moan came again and this time Deadalus was able to locate the source as a dark silhouette against the black of a tree. Deadalus approached cautiously. The sound had not been human.

A few meters from the tree Deadalus saw that it was one of the monkeys, seemingly hanging in mid-air. Again the monkey moaned. For a moment he considered turning away, his mind filled with all the possible dangers, but then he continued, drawn by the obvious pain in the sound.

The monkey was caught in a snare. It was hanging from a thin wire which was wrapped about its wrist. Its forearm was twisted at an awkward and painful angle. As he got close, Deadalus realized that the animal was unconscious.

The snare was evidently part of the pirate's fur-gathering. It was designed to catch the monkey with a minimum of damage to the pelt. Deadalus raised the laser preparing to kill the animal and end its agony. He paused, remembering the look of intelligence in the monkey the pirates were experimenting on. Perhaps it would be possible to let the trapped animal go. He considered for a moment, wondering if the animal would be able to survive with a broken arm, and then decided that he might as well give it a chance.

Quickly he cut through the wire with the laser and gently lowered the monkey down to the ground. The wire unwrapped from around its wrist, revealing a deep and ugly cut. He could perhaps bandage it, but the monkey would just as likely tear the bandage off the first chance it got. For that matter he could splint its arm as well.

Deadalus stood up, shaking his head. He didn't have time to stay here playing nursemaid to the animal. Angrily he turned and started back through the jungle.

Ten minutes later he paused, fighting with himself. He couldn't just leave the monkey there like that. The pirates were certain to find it when they came searching for him. He couldn't leave it there helpless to be tortured and slaughtered. He turned around and hurried back.

The monkey was just as he'd left it, still unconscious. Working quickly Deadalus cut down some branches to use as a splint. He wrapped some vines tightly around it to hold it in place. He was just about to bandage the animal's wrist when the monkey came to.

Deadalus quickly picked up his gun and stepped back. He didn't expect the animal to be overwhelmed with gratitude. The monkey's eyes were wide, watching him.

"It's OK, boy," Deadalus said soothingly. "You're alright now. I'm not going to hurt you."

In a quick move the animal rolled over and got into a crouch. Deadalus braced himself. The monkey investigated the splint on its arm, sniffing at it. For a moment he thought the monkey was going to pull it off. But after a few investigatory tugs, the animal seemed to realize that it would hurt to try and remove it. Turning its attention back to Deadalus, the monkey studied him with a look of perceptive intelligence.

"You're OK now. Just leave that splint alone and you'll be alright. Now go on. Shoo!" Deadalus waved his hands, motioning for the monkey to leave. But it crouched where it was, watching.

"Have it your own way." Deadalus turned and started away through the jungle, looking back over his shoulder. The monkey watched him for a minute and then turned and sprang up the tree. Deadalus watched, happy to see that the animal hardly seemed hampered at all by its splint. The monkey disappeared into the canopy of branches high overhead and Deadalus started back on his way.

After about an hour of picking his way through the vines Deadalus stopped. He was just too worn out to make any kind of progress. He would be better off if he could get some rest. He hated to take the time out, but he wasn't making any progress this way and his mind was so dull he wasn't thinking straight. He looked up at the interlocking branches which cut off the sky. Maybe it would be a good idea to follow the monkey's example.

Deadalus climbed up a tree until he reached the canopy which turned out to be mostly composed of thick vines that grew horizontally from tree to tree. The growth was so thick and tangled that Deadalus was unable to push his way through, and finally had to cut a section with his laser.

He climbed through and lay down, exhausted. The vines were like a nest and were as secure and comfortable as anything he could have hoped for. The sky above him was clear and cold, the stars standing out sharply against the velvet background.

Clutching the knife in one hand and the gun in the other, Deadalus fell asleep and dreamed of Clea, bathtubs, and dead bodies.

chapter seventeen

Deadalus opened his eyes. The sky was a pale, predawn gray. The canopy of branches stretched out around him like a great sea, here and there broken by the jut of a taller tree thrown up in black silhouette against the lightening sky. Deadalus listened, unable to credit the sound which had welled up across his subconscious to wake him. The sound came again.

Deadalus jerked up, every muscle taught. It seemed impossible, but the sound was unmistakable. It was a sound which, once heard, stuck with you for the rest of your life. It came again. It was the baying of hound dogs on the hunt.

He cursed and got to his knees on the thick sea of vines. As he did so, he picked up a motion among the limbs nearby. But when he turned quickly and looked he was unable to spot anything.

He pushed aside the worry over wild animals in order to think about his main problem. If the pirates were using dogs to track him, the headstart he'd gotten the night before was meaningless.

He checked the charge on the handgun and found, with disgust, that the gun was almost dead. He just about threw it away but then changed his mind and stuck it in his belt. Even if it had only one shot left that one shot would be better than nothing, and he had a suspicion he was going to need every bit of help he could get.

Looking around he took his bearings. He had been heading toward the ruins which he could see now at the edge of the jungle, standing out like an island in a calm sea. It seemed to him that the ruins would be a good place to try and set up an ambush. If he could get there in time. But first he'd backtrack a ways.

Crawling on his hands and knees Deadalus made his way over the canopy. His progress was painfully slow, but at least it would serve to throw the dogs off his trail for awhile. And he didn't expect to be able to use the maneuver for very long. As the sun came up over the tops of the trees he heard the sound he'd been expecting. Three small flyers were coming out from the fort.

Quickly he worked his way back down under the cover of branches. There was no way he could hide from the flyers up on top.

Deadalus sat amid the branches, catching his breath and considering what to do next. Suddenly he became aware that a monkey was watching him from nearby. The look in the animal's eyes was not friendly and Deadalus decided that he'd best vacate the trees. Immediately.

He ran as fast as he could through the vine

covered jungle but within a half hour he knew he wasn't going to make it to the ruins. The pack of dogs were moving too fast for him to outrun. He pushed himself still faster.

He was aware now that there were a number of monkies in the trees and that they appeared to be following him. He wasn't certain if they had any intention other than simple curiosity, but he didn't really care to find out.

The dogs were closing in fast. Evidently they were on some form of electronic leash where their progress could be monitored from a distance without having to be slowed down by the tracker's more difficult progress. Deadalus could hear them closing in. He'd have to try something to shake them off his trail.

Desperately he backtracked, circled around a tree, climbed up it, and then leapt out as far as he could. Ten minutes later he stopped to catch his breath and listen. The hounds had stopped their baying. Maybe they had lost his trail.

He caught his breath and started on. Two minutes later he suddenly realized his mistake.

The dogs burst through the shrubs a mere five yards behind him. They had stopped baying because they were no longer following his trail, they were following him. And they were closing in for the kill.

Deadalus dashed for the nearest tree. Monkies or not, he wasn't goin to stay and be torn apart by a pack of hunting dogs. He reached the tree, but the first dog was on him before he could pull himself up. As the dog leaped, Deadalus turned and blasted him with the laser.

The next dog leapt as the laser went dead. Deadalus threw the useless gun, momentarily stopping the dogs charge, and turned to desperately pull himself up out of reach. But even as his fingers scraped against the bark he knew he wasn't going to make it.

Then something unexpected happened.

Deadalus felt something drop past him out of the tree. There was an angry snarl and then a very pained yelp. Deadalus pulled himself up the tree before turning around to see what was happening.

Below him the pack of twenty or so hunting dogs were being attacked by four monkies. And the monkies were winning. With a strength which belied its size Deadalus saw one monkey pick a dog up by two of its legs and literally tear it in half. As he watched three more monkies swung through the trees and dropped down into the fray.

The monkies had now completely encircled the remaining dogs and were finishing them off with brutal efficiency.

As Deadalus turned back away from the slaughter something caught his eye. He looked closer. One of the monkies had something wrapped around its arm and, when the animal paused for a moment, Deadalus was able to see that it was the same monkey that he had helped from the trap.

Amazed and puzzled and more than a little thankful, Deadalus climbed up the tree until he was hidden in the branches overhead. The only option open to him now was to conceal himself the best he could and hope that the

pirates wouldn't be able to find him with the
dogs out of commission. He wasn't going to
venture down the tree with the fight still going
on and with the awful racket that they were
making he knew that who ever was following
the dogs was going to arrive before he had a
chance to run.

The fight lasted another five minutes and
the monkies were just finishing off the last
dog when a loud rifle shot sent them scattering through the brush, leaving one monkey
dead on the ground. There was another shot
and a second monkey fell from out of the trees.
Then there was silence. Deadalus waited.

Below him a pirate clad all in black came
out of the brush. He was carrying a long-
barreled, high-power projectile type rifle and
he stood looking over the bloody scene of battle.
The pirate looked up at the trees and Deadalus
was surprised to see that it was the pirate
leader himself.

Deadalus waited, watching as the man below him looked around with bemusement. One
minute ticked slowly by. Then another. A slow
smile began to spread across Deadalus's face.
It was becoming increasingly clear that the
pirate chief was alone.

It was such a stroke of good fortune that
Deadalus couldn't help but be suspicious. Yet
it fit in with everything he knew of the other's
character. The pirate boss was so sure of himself that he came alone with the hounds just to
better relish the sport of tracking him down
and killing him. An event which certainly
would have happened had not the monkies

intervened. But now the odds were suddenly less one-sided. The dogs were dead and the pirate was alone deep in the jungle, so far from the fort that, even if he had some means of calling them, it would take a long time for his men to reach him.

The black-clad pirate squatted down next to the last dog, which was still barely alive. He gently stroked its head and talked to it in a low voice. Then he stood up and quickly shot it. The bloody massacre of what were obviously prized dogs seemed to have distracted the pirate from his search for Deadalus. He walked from dog to dog, staring down at their mangled bodies.

Quietly, with a minimum of motion, Deadalus took out his knife and cut the end of one of the vines which stretched from tree to tree. Putting his knife between his teeth he held on to the vine with both hands and waited for the pirate to come into range. Then silently he dropped out of the tree, swooping toward the other Deadalus.

At the last moment the pirate caught the motion out of the corner of his eye and swung his rifle up, but it was too late. Deadalus hit the pirate feet first, sending the gun flying and tumbling them both to the ground. Deadalus rolled and came up, just as the pirate also sprang to his feet, a long two-sided knife in his hand.

The pirate's face was hard with fury, his lips drawn back from his teeth in a deathly grin.

"This is going to be a pleasure," the pirate

said as they warily faced each other, knives at the ready.

The pirate feinted but Deadalus moved out of reach. They began circling each other, looking for an opening. The footing was treacherous and the light poor. They thrust and parried and counter-thrust, neither getting any advantage over the other. Both men began sweating from the exertion; Deadalus could taste the salty perspiration on his lips and constantly had to shake his head to keep it out of his eyes.

Time seemed to drag to a halt. The pirate, who was at first extremely sure of himself, grew cautious as he realized his opponent's skill. For his part, Deadalus had never faced a man who so well matched his own fighting ability. He tried every trick he knew to breach the other's defenses, but it seemed that the better Deadalus fought, the better the other responded.

The pirate had talked at first, trying to distract Deadalus by telling him what he was going to do to him. But he had fallen quiet when he saw it was having no effect. Deadalus had remained absolutely silent. The fight continued.

Finally, Deadalus could feel his arm growing heavy and saw that his opponent was feeling the strain as well. Soon one of them would falter, an over extended thrust, a misjudged step, a feint not parried quickly enough, and the fight would be instantly over.

Deadalus dropped his arm lower, feigning a greater fatigue than he actually felt. He fought off the other's thrusts, making only a few slow thrusts of his own. He backed up constantly now, giving way before the pirate. Finally, dropping his arm even lower, he stepped back out of the others reach and spoke.

"You're giving a pretty good fight for someone who knows he's doomed. Or have you lost your faith in Clea's prediction?"

Feeling that Deadalus was nearly defeated, the pirate smiled.

"Clea has never been wrong. She said that Deadalus would kill Deadalus. And that is what's about to happen."

Deadalus took another carefully calculated step back and let his arm drop even lower.

"Oh?" he said with surprise. "Didn't she tell you the rest of it?"

Deadalus saw a spark of doubt flash across the pirate's face. His words had touched on a real fear. The pirate had known that Clea had held something back and now Deadalus's words pressed on him. He moved in to quickly finish Deadalus off. And he moved just a little too quick.

And the fight was suddenly over.

In taking that last step back Deadalus had stepped over a large puddle of blood which had settled in a low area under the vines. The puddle was not apparent unless one stepped in it, which Deadalus had done earlier in the fight. And now the pirate, in lunging too quickly, stepped in the puddle and slipped. His arm wavered as he tried desperately to keep his balance and in that instant Deadalus's knife was thrust home into the pirate's heart.

Sheer disbelief filled the man's face as he jerked back. His mouth formed a question, but he had no breath left to give it voice. With a look of eternal confusion, the pirate Deadalus dropped dead, the thick sea of undergrowth hushing the sound of his fall.

Deadalus waited until nightfall before attempting to board the pirate's ship. There was one man standing guard but Deadalus was able to easily pick him off with the high-powered rifle. He got to the communication room and quickly contacted the Orpheus.

"Captain?" It was Rhea's voice. "It's good to hear from you. Are you alright?"

"Yes. How close are you?"

"We're fourteen and a half minutes away."

"Good. There might be a space ship coming on you pretty soon, flying a white flag. Do not contact it. Blast it. Make absolutely certain it is completely destroyed. It's carring poison. Understand?"

"Yes sir."

"I don't know how much resistance you'll have in taking the fort here. There are two ships and the fort itself is no doubt armed. Don't take any undue risks, but don't do anymore damage than you have to."

"Yes sir. Where will you be?"

"I've a few things to attend to, but I should be out of the way by the time the fighting starts."

A sudden alarm sounded from the fort. Deadalus quickly cut the connection with the Orpheus and left the ship. He stopped momentarily to get the handgun from the guard he'd killed and then he hurried toward the jungle.

In a confused mass the pirates were running to their ships. Deadalus surmised that they had picked up the Orpheus on the radar and were hampered by their chief not being there to direct them. Keeping to the edge of the jungle in the dark he was able to make it to the fort without drawing any attention and, as the two ships blasted off Deadalus crossed the floodlit compound and ran in the open door.

He wanted to try and get the women and kids clear of the fort before the fighting began. He stopped a woman who was hurrying by and asked where he could find Clea and was directed upstairs to the laboratories. Keeping careful track so as not to get lost, he hurried through the twisted hallways. The warning siren had stopped and everything was suddenly quiet. Here and there Deadalus passed other women all hurrying down toward the basement of the building.

As he rounded a corner he collided with a young lady who was carrying a carton of food and supplies which she dropped, spilling the contents across the hall. Mumbling a quick apology to the startled girl, Deadalus stooped and helped her scoop the supplies back into the box. Just as he stood to hand the carton back to the young lady she screamed and ran off down the hall. He heard a laugh from behind him. His blood turned cold.

"Don't move too fast sweetheart or we might not get a chance to say goodbye."

Deadalus looked back over his shoulder. In the hallway behind him, holding a gun leveled on his midrift, was Syndy. Or what was left of her.

Her hair had been burnt off, her head and the sides of her face were black and blistered like a marshmellow that had fallen in a campfire. Her eyelids had been ripped off and her eyeballs stood out bare and red. Her left arm ended in a stump which was wrapped in a dirty and blood soaked rag. The few torn pieces of clothes left on her revealed similar torturous atrocities over the rest of her body but Deadalus could not bear to look. He looked only at her agonized, half-crazed eyes. And the unwavering gun.

His own gun lay on the floor where he had set it down while helping the girl. He had no chance what so ever of getting it. Even a poor marksman would be able to gun him down before he could reach it. And Syndy, he knew, was not a poor marksman. She was a fully trained agent of the secret police.

"Well, don't you have anything to say?" She said, grimacing and revealing a number of missing teeth. "After what we've been through together, Deadalus, I would think that you could at least offer some word of greeting. Or farewell."

Deadalus tried to reply, but the words stuck in his throat.

"Funny, isn't it?" she said in a strangely nonchalant manner. "I was sent to kill the traitor Deadalus. I was flattered. It was quite an honor to be considered skilled enough to tackle the famous ex-agent. And then I completely blow it by going after the wrong man. Tell me, did you know who I was all along? Did you just play with me and then tell the pirates who I was?"

Deadalus slowly shook his head in denial, not taking his eyes off the eyes of the once beautiful woman.

She studied him.

"No. That wouldn't be your style. Not only would that have been cruel, it would have been stupid. And you are neither cruel nor stupid. You want to know what's really funny? I wasn't just playing with you either. I think I really did fall in love with you. Why did you have to come back?"

As if in answer to her painful question an explosion rocked the building. There was an answering volly from some ground artillery.

Syndy sighed. "That would be your starship, wouldn't it? Well Deadalus dear, time is running out. There is one thing I want to know. Is the pirate, the one who did this to me, is he dead?"

Deadalus nodded.

"Well, I can thank you for that at least. Though I would have enjoyed doing it myself. I guess it's time to say goodbye sweetheart. Wish I could say it's been fun."

Another explosion rocked the building. The gaslights flickered and one went out. Deadalus did the only thing he could, even though he knew it was useless.

Throwing the carton of supplies at her he dove toward Syndy's feet. It was just a reflexive action from his long years of training. She would easily be able to shoot him two or three times before he reached her.

He heard the sound of the laser even as he dove. He could smell burnt flesh. But he couldn't feel anything. The expected blackness did not come. He wondered wildly if death could really be so painless.

He grabbed Syndy's legs but even as he did so he realized that she was already falling. Instead of trying to knock her down he found himself instinctively reaching out and catching her as she fell, limp and lifeless in his arms.

He knelt on the floor staring with numb confusion at the dead woman he held. Then he looked up.

Standing a dozen yards down the hallway, a laser gun in her hand, was Clea. Slowly, as if thinking itself had become difficult, Deadalus realized that he was alive and unharmed, that Clea had killed Syndy.

Clea stared back at him and in the flickering light it was impossible to read her features. Finally she spoke.

"I was listening. He's really dead?"

Deadalus nodded.

One right after the other three missiles hit the fort. The building shook to its foundation and from far off came the sound of collapsing stonework.

Slowly he lay Syndy down on the cold floor

and stood up. It was too late to get the women out of the building. He just hoped that they were as safe as they could get. Gently he took the unresisting Clea by the hand and led her down to the basement.

An hour later Deadalus was sitting in one of the Orpheus's landing crafts talking to Whisky while Jay administered to his wounds.

One of the pirate ships had been blown up but the other had escaped as the Orpheus concentrated on the castle. The resistance there had been very short-lived.

"So what are we to do about all the females?" Whiskey was asking. "Some of them even have children."

"We'll have to find room for them on the Orpheus tonight. Tomorrow we'll work out some method of getting them all back where they belong."

Clea, who had been standing unnoticed at the back of the cabin now spoke up.

"I for one don't want to leave. And I think alot of the others will say the same."

Deadalus looked at her surprised.

"What do you propose then?"

"This is a good planet. It's fertile and has many riches. And it is still free from the Empire."

"You think you can do it?"

"With your help. After what we've been through I don't think any of us will be afraid of a little hard work. Not when it means being free."

Deadalus looked at the light in her eyes and

he could feel something in him respond to the idea. To revive the dead planet, to rediscover the secrets of the society that had once lived here. And to learn from its mistakes.

Yes, it could be done. And probably should be done. The pirate Deadalus had discovered a number of things to use as weapons, how many things could be discovered that would be beneficial to mankind?

But the power was fearful. It was this power that had driven his evil counterpart to his dreams of galactical conquest. And, as the pirate had taught him, the line dividing good and evil was very thin at times. To try and set up a new Earth would run the risk of falling into the same mistakes of the old earth.

The greater amount of power that one had the greater was his ability to do either evil or good. Deadalus almost felt afraid of such power. He thought of his double and wondered if he would fall victim to the same horror that had invaded the pirate's heart.

Deadalus looked at Clea. He looked at Whiskey, Jay, and Rhea. It was a risk, but the possible good that could come from it was too great of an opportunity to pass up.

"Alright Clea. We can do it. We can set up a new society, free from the old mistakes, the old tyrants."

Deadalus stood up, feeling his weariness.

"But let's talk about it in the morning. Right now all I want to do is get something to drink and go to sleep."

"Shall I take us back up to the Orpheus?" Whiskey asked.

Deadalus walked to the open door of the landing craft and looked out.

"No. I've already got a room reserved here. It doesn't have much of a view, but the bed is soft."

He turned to ask Clea if she cared to come with him, but she was already right behind him.